GHOSTS

OF THE

FORBIDDEN

GLAZIER'S GAP BOOK 1

LEANNA RENEE HIEBER

CASTLE BRIDGE MEDIA
DENVER, COLORADO, USA

CASTLE BRIDGE MEDIA
Denver, Colorado

Cover photo by Katerina Klio/Shutterstock

This book is a work of fiction. Names, characters, business, events, and incidents are the products of the authors' imaginations. Any resemblance to actual persons, living or dead or actual events is purely coincidental.

GHOSTS OF THE FORBIDDEN
© 2022 Castle Bridge Media
All rights reserved.

ISBN: 979-8-9859702-1-0

65c  A Persephone Publications Gothic 25-64

by the author of
RIVER OF BLOOD

MARTHA GREEN

THE CURSE

We make ghosts
out of every
joy and sorrow
if we leave
any of them unsaid.

Prologue

Glazier's Gap, Colorado, 1979

MARTHA GREEN WAS CERTAIN SHE was alone in the cavernous mansion. So, when an arched door creaked on its hinges as it opened down the hall, revealing only darkness beyond, her frayed nerves slipped along a precarious thread towards an irrecoverable abyss.

The darkened, disorienting mansion of endless additions and frenetic design that sprawled out around her felt suddenly close. Only sporadic sconces were lit, disconcerting patches of light and darkness. She ran through a windowless ballroom, past an unsettling anteroom full of taxidermized creatures and finally to the library where she'd been told a treasure awaited her. Once she picked it up, her job would be done and she would be on her way, leaving this strange little town to occupy its own liminal space.

Glazier's Gap changed people, for better or for worse and she wasn't really sure which one had been happening to her.

The mansion library, which also served as the archive room for Persephone Publications, was locked. Martha looked behind her nervously as she fumbled a 19th century key into a stubborn lock. Only deep shadows sat in stillness. A bold shaft of light coming in from an unexpected skylight illuminated the stuffed lion staring at her from the anteroom, one paw raised. Had it always been poised like that?

The town didn't just change people. Things changed too. As if nothing was quite as you remembered it. Subtle shifts of angle or detail. She had no idea how she'd managed to write a novel in such an environment but any time that she couldn't quite trust her senses, she had credited it to the unreliable narrators who drove her story. The excuse wasn't a comfort now.

The door finally gave way and Martha rushed into a brightly painted room where everything was lavishly rococo in style but done in bold contemporary shades. Glass-paneled bookshelves went floor to ceiling around the perimeter, desks interrupting them at intervals, a quartet of settees for reading and lounging held court in the center of the wide space carpeted in green shag.

Three porthole skylights cast circular shafts of light down into the peculiar space. She crossed into a shaft as she approached the furthest desk from the door. The large, open rolltop with a wingback chair before it was where the owner of Persephone Publications liked to run things, though it had been months since she'd been back in town.

As her editor had promised, a book sat on the dusty surface of the desk; a finished copy having just come in from the binder and unboxed for her. Martha set her clutch purse down on the desk and picked up the copy in eager hands, drinking in its details. The cover depicted a Gothic mansion not dissimilar to the one she was in, with a light on in a tower and a woman in a gauzy gown, fleeing down a dim, forested lane, the palette of blues and golds sharply contrasting shadow and light.

THE CURSE, by Martha Green.

"We make ghosts out of every joy and sorrow if we leave any of them unsaid," Martha murmured the tagline of the book. It sounded suddenly strange, as if she'd just foretold a prophecy.

She ignored that the temperature in the room plummeted an unnatural degree. Instead, she turned the hardcover over in her hands, relishing the smooth feel of the dust jacket and the sight of her name in bold letters.

"Release day, little story," she said to the book. "I release you into the world and I hope some old wounds can heal. Be well, Camille and William.

Close your chapter, dear hearts."

Martha turned to go, about to grab her purse when her breath and her heart seized. In the thin layer of dust across the lacquered desk, a shaking finger had written:

DON'T LEAVE THE HOUSE

It had not been there just moments before.

She recoiled, her book tumbling from her hands.

Sure, she'd written about the town lore; how the Glazier mansion allegedly contained certain protections that didn't seem to apply anywhere else, but what could anything or anyone want with her? Threats and animosity were all as dead and buried as the old hatchets cast between the Glazier and Denny families a century prior. Fumbling for the book, then her purse, she faced the warning as she retreated towards the door, as if she didn't dare turn her back on it.

But she did have to go. She had a flight to catch and with traffic, she was already pressing her luck. A life awaited her back home in New York. She shut the library door behind her and darted back the way she'd come, pausing at the great wooden front doors of the mansion, enormous beasts, detailed in silver filigree mined from the family's own local operations in the mountain.

Something a town bartender had said to her came to mind. She'd been sitting poring over page-proofs at The Blue Taper, the bar adjacent to the abandoned ski resort that somehow was always bustling even though everything around it was dead. He'd whistled soft and low and shook his head when she'd told him the general plot.

"Good thing the Denny family isn't around this time of year. They won't like you dragging that old story into the light. Great grandma said they always had a mean streak."

"It's fictionalized—"

"They'll know. Somehow, they always knew if someone had been talking about them. The Denny family may have been cursed but I guarantee you, the curse cut both ways. Someone always paid for an insult or injury, one way or another."

Shrugging it off with a sip of a martini, she'd finished her edits and hadn't thought anything more about it. Superstition was rife and she didn't believe in old wives' tales or in the paranormal explanations locals had ascribed to the town's disasters and economic downturns.

Shaking her head now, she convinced herself she hadn't seen anything unusual inside, that it was just the anxious effects of her ongoing insomnia. She heaved open the great doors, tossed her set of office keys through the silver mail slot and set off down the long steep lane towards the town below, where she'd gather her bags and hire a car.

Her heels clicked sharply on the uneven asphalt. The usual birds in the trees had gone silent. The bright day had turned darker than when she'd gone inside. Sirens in the distance were coming closer. A plume of smoke could be seen past the thicket of Douglas firs that lined Glazier Drive. If she wasn't mistaken, one of the historic buildings she'd written about—fictionalized— was on fire.

She picked up her pace until she saw the figure. Stopping abruptly, she wavered on her feet. Her body went ice cold under her sweater and pencil skirt.

A figure stood at the end of the drive, some ten yards ahead of her, framed by a fire behind it. Tall and oddly shaped, the dark silhouette in a black frock coat with shining eyes set deeply in a shadowed face began approaching, limping its way towards her, up the narrow lane. Its fingers were long— too long, hanging on either side of gangly arms like blades. The figure reached out a long, deadly hand.

The towering fir trees that covered the lane in shadow spun in Martha's vision as she collapsed to her knees, then pitched to the side, clutching at her chest as it exploded in pain, and everything went dark.

Someone always paid for a curse, one way or another.

Chapter One

Present Day, Manhattan

AN ENVELOPE EXCLAIMING "YOU'RE INVITED" in scrawling red ink was slid under the door of Lillian Anders' small studio apartment. She'd been crying but stopped abruptly upon sight of the paper, her heart beginning to race instead.

"What the..." She dried her eyes on the black lace cuff of her dress, marring charcoal eyeliner across her pale hand. Approaching the envelope cautiously, she nudged it with her black ballet flat, as if making sure it was dead. She pointed at the intruder and addressed it sharply. "I have had a *bad* day, whatever you are."

She stared at the envelope for a moment before darting to her apartment door, throwing it open only to hear the front door, five flights down, click shut. Shaking her head, she closed her door and stared again at the bold invitation.

A whisper sounded somewhere. Something tickled the back of her mind, like a memory taking hazy shape.

For all 35 years of her restless life, she'd looked for things out of the corner of her eye; sure, there was something just out of frame that she wasn't catching but should. She grabbed the envelope, turned it over, and opened the red wax seal with a heraldic crest of three candlesticks with lit tapers.

Calling all Gothic Writers

Persephone Publications Lives Again

Help us celebrate the revival of a premier Gothic Publisher of the 20th
Century in historic, picturesque, quirky Glazier's Gap, Colorado!
Come brainstorm ideas for new novels…
Join a talented group of women writers for an all-expenses paid retreat!

An email for Bethany Glazier and a publishing website followed at the end of the looping script and that was the end of it. The name sort of rung a bell but Lillian had no idea why or how a publishing invite from Colorado was hand-delivered under her Washington Heights studio door. She was goth, and had been since she was a teen, but that didn't imply some kind of national, automatic bat-signal. How did this reach her?

Holding the invite, she could have sworn she felt something. On her shoulder. A push. A hand. A nudge…

Swiftly, she chided herself. "No. You're thirty-five. With a thirteen-year-old's overactive imagination…"

But the corner of her mind that was *sure* otherworldly capabilities lay buried within her began testing its surroundings; a long-dormant dragon waking up from under a mountain.

Lillian grabbed her phone and dialed her dearest, most grounded friend. It was always good for a person with chaotic alignment to have at least one designated practical associate. The moment Keri picked up the line, Lillian launched into a torrent:

"I have had, categorically, the hardest day of my life. I finally ended it with Brad, we're done for good, the Marley House is replacing all its guides with pre-recorded tours and closing its research library—so there go my jobs—and I've just lost rent control on this damnable shoebox."

Keri paused. "Yes. That's worst day material. I'm just up the block, I'll turn around, grab some wine. You get the envelope?"

"You mean the heart-attack slid under my door? That was you?"

Keri laughed. "I figured you'd love that wizard-school nonsense! Oh, no, sorry, I should have written *'E. F. Rochester of Thornfield Hall'* in the top left corner instead," she taunted. "But I think you should go on the retreat! Especially now since you have no job, no boyfriend, soon no home—its providence!"

"Your 'look on the bright side' is--"

"Why you called me." Keri set the phone down and Lillian heard chatter over the bodega register before she picked it back up and doorbells jingled in her wake. "It's what you need right now. You've told me yourself: depressed goths are a tired stereotype."

Lillian sighed. In a moment, her door buzzed, and she let Keri in downstairs and opened her door as her friend climbed the rickety stairs. Soon, a curly-haired woman with a warm light brown complexion, dressed in a colorful, stylish dress, entered with a bag. She handed over the bottle, looking at her friend warily.

"You look like The Crow, Lilli. I know that's often what you're going for—but *this* smudged eyeliner is from tears, not artfully crafted in vengeance. Correct me if I'm wrong."

"You are not wrong. Please. Help me out of existential crisis."

"Have some Wine Product. Bodega's finest."

Lillian poured dangerously sweet Sangria into red glass goblets, dumped corn chips into a skull bowl, deposited them on a black-lacquer coffee table and flounced onto a velvet-draped armchair.

"So. All the things you thought might happen did," Keri prompted, making herself comfortable on a worn brocade settee Lillian had enlisted friends to help seize off the street; New York often providing unexpected curbside treasures. "You knew the new director of the museum might automate, Brad hasn't actually been *hearing* you in, what, I don't know how long, and this building is falling apart under your feet. I say good riddance to all of it. I'm not being callous; I just think you've been treading water. I think you deserve more."

"Thank you. And yes, all of these things are true. But I don't want to go back to St. Paul. Nothing against home—save for the snow—I just... I just want to feel like I'm moving forward in life."

"Take this retreat!" Keri exclaimed. "I would if I could. The invite came to me, Bethany is dear a friend from girls' school, she's curated a great team. I took the liberty of sending her your posts for the museum. She likes your style; the way you craft atmosphere in historical non-fiction frameworks."

"Oh. Well. Thank you." Lillian was deeply moved her friend had gone to the trouble.

"You've told me before that you felt like something was missing. Like there was something you were supposed to find, here, in New York. What if it isn't here? What does *home* feel like to you now, when you think about it?"

It was, Lillian had to admit, a really good question. "You know, one of the reasons I was always so obsessed with Jane Eyre is something about it felt like home. The era. Did I ever tell you when I was little, I'd sometimes get confused by cars, by phones? My parents said I'd 'phase out,' like I'd forget I was in the 20th century. '1987 going on 1887', they'd say if I ever talked about my birth year and feeling out of place."

"That concept, in and of itself, would make a great story for Persephone Press, seriously," Keri offered. "They excelled in 70s Gothic novels. Go run from a crumbling manor house in your nightgown with a candelabra. The stuff of legend. The old Glazier mansion itself is wild, Bethany showed me pictures. I can't tell if it's beautiful or a creepy film still. Maybe both. The town is quirky and stuck in the past."

"Like me?"

Keri smiled. "Why else would I think of you?"

"Will you help me write an email to Bethany?"

"Or I can text her right now. Do a video chat. I told her I'd be inviting you on her behalf today."

"Wow. You are--"

"On. It."

Taking action was exactly what was needed, and Lillian was grateful for the distraction. She may be goth, but she wasn't emo.

Within minutes there was an invite in Lillian's inbox.

"Let me fix my face," Lillian said, plucking an eyeliner pencil from a

10

mug by a cracked oval mirror. Staring at her reflection; dark brown hair, too-pale skin, sharp cheekbones and huge smudged dark circles under her eyes, she looked a fright—and not the carefully-crafted kind.

Breathing deeply, trying to appreciate her own face for its distinct quirks and imperfections, she wiped the charcoal liner into place, letting the smudged effect around her eyelids stay but removing all the black traces of tear stains from her cheeks, finishing up with a dark burgundy lip gloss.

"Ok." Lillian sat down at her desk, and clicked the link to the video call, adjusting the camera view on her laptop, centering herself before a large-framed print of Edvard Munch's *Love and Pain*—often called *The Vampire* after its red-haired subject bending over a dark-haired lover—that hung on the wall behind her.

Bethany Glazier came onto screen; a pretty Asian woman with long black hair and a red ruffled blouse that was a bright contrast to her background: a huge, dark room with arching rafters of dark wood and a lit fireplace at the side of the screen. There was a strange, silvery mist floating behind her, a neat digital background effect.

"Hi Lillian! I'm Bethany, thanks for taking the call."

"Thanks for having me. I'm definitely intrigued, and I'd love to know more about the retreat." She left out "because I have no other options in life right now" as it didn't sound very professional. "What all would you be looking for from me?"

"We'd love to get a whole bunch of pitches, page-long synopses, story seeds, thoughts on what kinds of re-imaginings we could do. We'll also be reissuing some of our best backlist titles in revised editions with introductions. I don't want to impose a specific word-count or product goal, but the more the better. We've got at least five women confirmed as attendees. You can stay here in one of the wings that's been renovated or in the carriage house, whichever you like the feel of best, no one has claimed any rooms yet."

"Ok," Lillian tried to appear nonchalant, but the truth was, she was excited about the idea.

"Keri also mentioned you've done some historic preservation work," Bethany continued. "Our archive is a mess. If you'd like to spend time helping me figure it out, I'd pay an hourly rate for your time. There's so much material, you could stay on after the retreat if you liked."

Lillian's heart surged. An actual job sounded great right about now.

"That's a *great* idea and I think Lillian should totally take you up on that," Keri popped her head into the frame next to Lillian, who smiled at her friend and nodded her agreement. "Hi Bethany!" Keri waved.

"Hello!" Bethany waved and blew a kiss. "Miss you! Wish you were coming out too!"

"I know, but non-profits *never* rest. Someday. Keep a candle in the window for me!" Keri popped back out of the frame.

"What got you into wanting to revive the publishing house?" Lillian asked.

"My mother wasn't always welcomed by everyone in the Glazier family, at least not right away. I could tell—kids can always tell—which relatives accept them fully and which don't. My parents' marriage wasn't why the publishing house closed, that was an economic situation before their time, but when it was handed to my father in my grandmother's will, they asked if I, as a writer, had any interest in it. Mom and Dad had no intention of leaving New York so it was a matter of taking up the reins or letting the whole thing leave the family entirely. So, I gathered some investors and figured I'd take a shot at it. I've noticed that very few publishing CEOs are people of color, so I'd like to be at least one representative voice in the industry."

"I absolutely want to support that."

"Good. What are some of your favorite themes? I noticed in your museum essays you focused a lot on changing class consciousness in the 19th century."

"Yes, that would be my main interest, every other specialty or niche stems from that."

"Ok, I think one of our titles even addresses that with its main characters. In a star-crossed-lovers kind of way. I've been trying to scan our backlist, it's a lot of titles to digitize but I'll send you the one I'm thinking of so you can get a sense of what Persephone used to publish. They're definitely Gothics of their era but they're fun. If you look for it, there's socioeconomic commentary within, plus winks and nods in the right places. We'll want to continue with that same kind of feel."

Bethany held up the book to the camera. It was a typical seventies-era Gothic with a running woman with windswept hair tearing away from a foreboding manor. THE CURSE was written boldly in huge letters.

The silvery mist that had been hanging behind Bethany in her digital background coalesced into a figure that began approaching the camera.

"That looks… fun…" Lillian said, trailing off as a truly *beautiful* man in a long cloak—his collar open as if he'd torn at his cravat in anguish—came into phantasmagorical focus. Luminous hair wild, he stared into the camera, directly at Lillian. Whatever fingernail had tapped at the back of her mind now began to dig in and scratch.

"Wow. Your digital background is sensational!" Lillian exclaimed, impressed, ignoring the fact that the ghost looked familiar. Surely some movie effect imported from something she'd watched long ago. "That ghost is… I have to say, *incredibly* attractive."

Keri poked her head in frame. "Holy shhhhh… that is… freaky."

Bethany whirled to look behind her. When she turned back, her mouth was slack, and her eyes were wide. "I don't have any background going, though…"

Lillian stared at the screen. Bethany looked behind her again, warily, then back to the camera. She seemed to be telling the truth.

"Oh…" Lillian chuckled nervously. "Then I… Ok."

"Nope! Nope!" Keri jumped to her feet, recoiling from the screen. "Nope. Not watching anymore, love y'all but no," Keri removed herself, refilled her wine glass and sat, wide-eyed, as far as distance could allow from the screen in Lillian's small studio.

"I don't see anything," Bethany insisted. "You're just messing with me!"

"No, I saw what I saw," Keri called. "Lillian will be fine, continue!"

"Yes, I'm… fine, I'm sure I'm just seeing a weird trick of the light," Lillian said, having a hard time not staring at the beautiful ghost that in no way could be excused as firelight or shadows. "But what room *are* you in? It's huge!"

"I'm… at a card table set up in the ballroom. It's a serious quirk of the house, that the room with no windows gets the best connection."

Bethany visibly shivered. The ghost wafted back but kept staring at

13

Lillian. It was an effort to break away from his gaze, but she didn't want anyone to get more scared, herself included. She wanted to change the subject but couldn't help herself and blurted: "I'm… sure you get asked a lot about whether the mansion is haunted."

Bethany shrugged. "Any old house has people thinking its haunted. I've not seen anything, you seeing something is a first, at least for me. But also, I've not felt any bad vibes here either," she added hastily.

"That's good!"

There was a brief silence. The breathtaking ghost faded further back into the shadows and Lillian felt her heart skip a beat, as if she didn't want him to go. She shook her head and asked Bethany about travel dates.

They discussed a few more details, Lillian liking Bethany immediately. She hoped they'd become friends through the process.

Just as Lillian and Bethany were signing off, the ghost swooped close, and the screen went entirely grey.

A man's voice pleaded: "Do you remember me?"

Lillian's screen blinked into the "meeting has been ended by host" window.

"NOPE!" Keri cried from the corner of the apartment. "That ghost did *not* just talk to you—tell me that was a pop-up ad--"

Lillian clasped her hands together, her heart thumping in her ears. "No… not an ad… Think it was the ghost--"

"That is ALL you, my friend. Have at it." She crossed herself. When Lillian cocked her head at her, she fired back. "I'm Episcopalian but I'm not taking any chances!"

Lillian laughed.

The two discussed logistics of moving Lillian's modest things into storage—she had more books than anything else. Her countless long black dresses of various fabrics; those would be hardest to part with.

Her inbox dinged and it was an email from Bethany with a PDF of THE CURSE by Martha Green. Lillian looked forward to reading it.

"You can write your own take on any of the classics," Keri said, eager to move on from the ghost. "You could do your own versions of your favorite Victorian dramas and highlight the social dynamics, class struggles, all the deep *secrets* in society, when no one was listening to one another--"

"Yes! Like, *Dracula*, for instance! The Count was the only one really listening to Mina, if you think about it, everyone else is just taking *around* her, all these men trying to decide her fate. Dracula, he was the only one who cared--"

"This may be *the* most goth thing you've ever said."

Lillian smiled. "Escalation is sometimes a necessary part of the creative process."

Keri's smile faded and she took a long draught of sangria. "I don't want to get freaked out again by what we just saw but… I'd have warned you if I *knew for sure,* that the place was haunted. Are you okay with that? I mean, goth stereotypes aside--"

"I've never seen anything manifest so clearly as that ghost did. That was wild. But weird stuff happened at the museum all the time. I just chalked it up to it being an old house that makes noises, has drafts and a lot of deep shadows." Lillian shrugged. "If I don't like the feel of the place, I'll leave."

"I'll send you some sage and holy water, just for good measure."

"You're good to me."

"Somebody's gotta be. Let's get your stuff together *now*. If I know Bethany, she'll find a travel voucher and get you out there within a week. You'd better be ready for that hot ghost!"

"Born ready."

They laughed, embraced and Keri was on her way to dance class.

Alone again, Lillian took a deep breath, her mind spinning with the events of the day. She looked out her window facing downtown. She watched the block around her, a microcosm of movement within the greater, constant ebb and flow of the island; a vast, complicated, breathing organism. She had such respect for the city, but it just wasn't home anymore. She wasn't sure it ever had been. A good place for a restless person, it had been a place to get lost in. But maybe she wanted, now, to be found.

She almost opened the document and started reading but her heart started galloping at an alarming rate and she closed her inbox instead. After dinner, a call to her parents, who were impressed she got a job the same day she lost one, had her thinking that maybe fate was looking out for her.

The nearly seven up-and-down years she'd spent with Brad, who'd always been far more focused on his career in academia than in maintaining their relationship, suddenly seemed far away, behind glass. One mostly empty shelf in the exhibit of her life. She had so much room, now, to grow.

By the end of the night, as she lay back listening to the myriad sounds of Manhattan, she heard something else, too: that ghost's aching voice in a whisper against her ear.

Do you remember me?

No. But she wanted to.

Chapter Two

ON A PLANE WITH EVERYTHING she could reasonably pack in two suitcases and the rest of her modest, scraping-by-life in storage, Lillian picked up her tablet and opened the scanned copy of THE CURSE.

As she began to read, the story focusing at first on young, shy, big-hearted Caroline Dennis, she soon got motion sick and had to put the tablet down and close her eyes. It might not have only been the turbulence, though. Something about Caroline felt familiar and Lillian couldn't fathom why. Stylistically, the language of the novel was a bit more florid than would be Lillian's preference in a 20th century piece, but there was a great deal of passion in the narrative from the start. The author's care for the characters was palpable and realistic, as if she were writing about people she knew; people who had really lived.

Having hardly rested the night prior due to nerves, Lillian managed to sleep most of the flight out.

Touching down, she texted Bethany, collected her bags and headed for the gate where Bethany had a car service waiting. She found a black car with ANDERS written in the window and a college-aged woman who had been hired as her driver hopped out and helped her with her bags. Setting off, the driver began pleasant, sporadic conversation but wasn't pushy. Lillian was glad to enjoy the new surroundings without constantly being asked questions or urged into small talk. The distant hills as seen from the airport began to rise into mountains as they drove.

Making a big turn towards a densely forested pass, the driver made a comment. "I admit I've actually never been into Glazier's Gap. My mom was born there and talks about the avalanche a lot, as it really scared her. Their house was damaged, and they moved to Estes Park, where my dad's wealthier relatives lived. But she said it was a really... interesting place, so I hope you have fun there!"

The young woman was cheery, but the way she paused before "interesting"—the way you'd pause before trying to say something nice about something you didn't like—was telling.

The colors out here were different from her experiences in Minnesota or New York, there was a different richness to the land. A particular turn revealed a slope of aspens blazing in full golden glory, bordered by verdant green conifers; the colors all the more intense for the contrast. Lillian gasped in appreciation. Her driver told her all the best spots in Rocky Mountain National Park that she *had* to see.

The moment the car turned onto the narrow road marked "Glazier Drive" on a fading, bent street sign, Lillian's heart started racing again. Huge Douglas fir trees were densely packed on either side of the lane until it all opened up onto an enormous, rocky plateau with an oval roundabout and the Glazier Mansion dominating the scenery.

"Wow," Lillian and the driver said at the same time.

A huge, sprawling Richardson Romanesque mansion in dark red sandstone with somewhat crazed, mis-matched Victorian and early 20th century additions was set against dramatic rock scaling back up behind it, almost as if the house was a fantastical outgrowth of the mountain itself. Lillian's heart hadn't stopped pounding. Staring at this house, her emotions grew loud, a groundswell of sentiment bubbling up inside her.

It was, she supposed, like she was *coming home* to Thornfield Hall, or any number of grand mansions she'd dreamed about in her favorite 19th century Gothics. Of course, she'd be emotional. That it felt familiar was just because it was such a wonderful example of her favorite architecture from her favorite era.

Bethany, dressed in a sharp black suit with a bright blue blouse, black hair up in a bun, was sitting on a bench outside the house reading a book when the car pulled under the wide, arched portico. "Hi Lillian!" She called as Lillian opened the car door. Bethany approached with a smile. "So glad you got in without a hitch!"

Bethany took care of payment with a generous tip and the driver was on her way, wishing everyone good luck with their new ventures.

"So. Bring your bags in. Since you're the first one here, you get first dibs on a room."

Lillian's eye was drawn to the side of the house, to a structure some thirty yards separate; a red brick and brownstone carriage house with a score of arched windows and a cozy feel, a curving line of holly bushes with bright berries surrounding it like an embrace. Her heart swelled. Tears suddenly limned her eyes. She wondered what had come over her. Must be near that time of the month.

Bethany was already in the entrance hall with one of Lillian's bags and she trotted ahead with the other to catch up.

The front entrance hall was long, dividing off left and right in an enormous length. Ahead of them, a cavernous foyer was adorned in rich, dark, carved mahogany with a carved wooden staircase leading to an upper level.

"Leave your bags here, I'll show you the rooms that are renovated and safely livable, there's the carriage house too. Not everything is open, not everything is cleaned or upkept, doors are locked, or things are closed off if that's the case."

"It's amazing. I... It's got so many of my favorite things. The grand stair, the inlaid wood, the fretwork, the carved wood paneling, even the wrought-iron ventilation grates. It's just all such beautiful craftsmanship."

"The house will appreciate your attention to its detail. I still haven't seen any ghosts like you did on screen—Oh God, though, are you seeing any now?" Bethany said, biting her lip and looking around warily.

Lillian chuckled and shook her head. "I'm not terribly sensitive, at least, I don't think. I'm not seeing anything here. Do you want me to tell you if I do, though?"

"Yes, I think so. I need to know everything to expect here."

As they reached the second-floor landing, they stepped into the hallway and onto blue shag carpeting that was completely at odds with the mahogany wood paneling. Gilt-trimmed paintings of still lives and landscapes marched along flocked wallpaper. The blue carpet matched blue resin candelabras cast in an imitation-Victorian pattern which hung at intervals from the ceiling, sporting a few flickering, faux-fire lightbulbs, most of them needed replacing.

"Well…" Lillian's heel caught on the thick shag.

"Yeah, don't mind the obnoxious 70s moments, you'll be going along beautifully in the mid-19th century and then suddenly its disco and peacock colors, I can't figure it. But all the money's going into the publishing house so the antithetical 20th century additions will have to stay as is."

"It's… got character."

"It *is* a character. And all I can do is to try to understand it and upkeep it as best anyone knows how. Thankfully, one of the old caretakers of the place under my grandma's watch, he and his son have agreed to come by once a week and do maintenance."

Lillian nodded. This house was part Addams Family, part kitsch, part legitimate Victorian masterpiece, like a quirky grand dame who had lived through so many decades and collected so many stories she was a trip at parties, especially when drunk.

Along the second-floor hallway a series of open doors marched ahead of them. All the rooms were finely appointed in dark colors, some of them in unaltered Victorian, others in a 70s palette version of a Victorian, with a four-post bed, a dresser, desk and one arched window looking out onto the lane below. From the windows, further down below, Glazier's Gap itself could be glimpsed as a collection of a few intersections and unique structures poking spires or lit signs out from among the trees.

"Any of the rooms in particular calling to you?" Bethany asked.

Lillian paused. "Did you say that the carriage house was also available? Not that I don't love the house, I mean, it's amazing, I just…"

"I think the light is better in there, to tell you the truth. Sometimes the hulking dark of this place gets to me."

"It isn't the dark, I mean, look at me," she gestured to her long black dress with a laced bodice and embroidered tracery, "I like the dark, it's just... I know this sounds weird but it... feels familiar."

"It's open, take a look around and see what will suit you." Bethany led her back down to the front door as she continued. "You'll be here longer than the others if you do want to take up the archival work, so I really want you to be comfortable! The mansion front door is open if you want to come back in and choose something upstairs instead, just take your time. I'll be over here in the parlor." She gestured at an angle to an open door to the side of the entrance foyer.

"Thank you so much. You've been... so great."

Bethany just smiled. "Being a host is my favorite thing! I love that this place is big enough to shelter a bunch of artists and writers. That's why I couldn't let it go."

"I love that you didn't! I'll come back to you soon."

"Oh, before I forget, here's the hardcover of the book I sent you. I know you've got the PDF but there's something about the book itself..." Bethany moved to a bench by the front door and held up a copy of *The Curse* with its bold, gold letters and frightened woman in a period gown mid-flight, looking back at a gloomy mansion.

"Thank you..." Lillian moved to pick it up from Bethany and the volume felt electric in her hands. She took it with her, leaving her bags behind until she made her choice.

Once outside, Lillian had to stop herself from running towards the smaller building, having no idea what had gotten into her.

The carriage house had been renovated into something warm and welcoming. Stepping inside, Lillian felt a profound thrill of anticipation that swept up her spine in a delicious tingle.

It was an open-plan space with a kitchen, wood cabinets, appliances and counters on one side with a long line of windows and beautiful wooden shutters in warm rosewood, a long wooden dining table sat against the opposite wall which was similarly bountiful with windows and shutters. A large sofa and cushioned wing-backed armchairs sat at the center of the open space facing an enormous fireplace with a wide stone mantel, a sumptuous floral-patterned rug splayed out before it. Lillian was delighted that there was already a fire lit in the huge, old hearth. She was surprised she hadn't smelled the firewood—always one of her favorite scents.

Beyond sliding wooden doors up a small flight of stairs sat the bedroom, bath and large closets, with an alcove desk area with a printer and office supplies. This was the place. Lillian walked the perimeter, running her hand over windowsills and along the lace table-runner, noting two hefty silver candelabras as centerpieces.

Turning back to the center of the room, she was about to sit before the fire a moment with *The Curse* and maybe read a few pages, but she stopped cold. The book slid from her hand and bounced to rest on the nearby armchair.

The fireplace was no longer lit. Not even smoking. As if it hadn't been lit at all.

Before she could puzzle over this further, two loud and brightly dressed women with obnoxious designer purses and huge sunglasses entered the carriage house, laughing. They stopped, startled by Lillian's presence.

They looked her up and down in her black, renaissance-style dress and choker, silent judgements unmistakably readable on their faces.

"Hiiii…" One of the blondes exclaimed. "I'm Cindy. This is Sally. Are you the help?"

"No." Lillian said flatly. "My name is Lillian. I'm here for the writer's retreat."

"Ah…" Sally seemed pained by this.

"You?" Lillian asked.

"We're cousins, here for the retreat too, our family angel-invested in the publishing house!" Cindy seemed to be waiting for applause or something.

"Ah…" Lillian echoed Sally's pained tone.

"So…" Sally looked her up and down again, pointedly. "You look like you know a thing or two about the dead. What are the most haunted spots in this town?"

Lillian shrugged. "I just got in an hour ago and know nothing about the place. I'm sure there will be time to explore before we start writing."

"Oh, I don't know about *writing*, that's boring. We're *influencers*," Cindy explained. "Our channel subscribers just topped two million, and we've *got* to get some content out here in the middle of nowhere. We've got to make this place look... cool. It will be some effort."

Lillian had to bite her tongue to keep from firing back that it was already cool. It certainly didn't need their valley-girl help.

"People *love* haunted places," Cindy explained, as if Lillian—or everyone—wasn't already very aware of this fact. "*Especially* ones they don't have access to."

At this, Lillian just nodded. It wasn't up to her to enforce which rooms and areas around the Glazier mansion were off-limits, but she suddenly felt the need to warn Bethany.

"Well, we've got footage to catch. See you around, Lil!" Cindy called, moving to the door, Sally on her heels.

"It's Lillian," she countered as they slammed the door behind them. Lilli was only for family and people she liked. *Lil* was for no one. For all that had gone smoothly thus far, it was only a matter of odds and timing for something to irritate her, and catty bitches certainly fit that bill. Lillian watched as they drove off in a fancy car, speeding down the narrow lane.

Pausing at the threshold, hand on the doorknob, about to go out to tell Bethany she'd picked the carriage house and get her bags, she stopped and looked behind her. The bedroom doors she'd pulled back closed had slightly slid open again. Must be the foundations settling and a latch not catching. She had to remind herself things were always shifting in old houses.

She returned to the Glazier mansion, noting how the angle of the house against the rising ridge behind it swallowed her in shadow the moment she neared its doorstep.

"I'd worried you'd gotten lost!" Bethany said as Lillian knocked on the open parlor door. The room was the brightest in the house she'd seen so far, it's furnishings in pastel brocades and cherry wood with a line of windows with golden floral stained-glass medallions in the corners that let in light from the clearing beyond. "What did you pick?"

"Carriage house, thank you!"

She thought about mentioning the fire. And the cousins. But she decided to just hold her tongue. No need to sound like an unreliable narrator—or a high-schooler complaining about the 'popular girls'—right out of the gate.

"We'll meet for dinner at six and start our first brainstorming session," Bethany explained.

"Great!" Grabbing her suitcases, Lillian returned to the carriage house to unpack.

She peeked around the corner of the front entrance landing to see if the fire was lit. It was not. It had to have just been her imagination. Not sleeping well did affect vision. Maybe it was causing hallucinations.

With some extra time before dinner, she wanted to get more of *The Curse* read, having felt like she'd neglected her homework.

The tagline of the book caught her breath; a note about ghosts being made out of unsaid things. She agreed. Ghosts could be countless things beyond mere spirit and form. Dreams. Regrets. Hopes. Roads not taken. Metaphors and consequences. How many different types were here in this town? How many did she, knowingly or unknowingly, hold in her heart?

She continued reading. The heroine, Caroline, began sneaking out at night to meet a lover. They discussed the impossibility of their love in fraught conversations. She, a lady, and he, a mere servant, could never be together. A plan was hatched to escape. Their passion was pure. The narrative dug in at points about class restrictions being poisonous and the lack of women's agency in centuries prior, underscoring florid prose with solid social commentary from the characters themselves.

Before she knew it, a small clock on the mantel chimed softly, a lovely antique in brass and filigree. Time to dine in the mansion.

Chapter Three

IN THE TIME SINCE LILLIAN arrived, other writing retreat participants were making their way in and had clearly been in the midst of unpacking.

Once the group of six were assembled in the foyer, women of all different backgrounds, shapes and styles, Bethany led everyone past the parlor and towards the dining room that lay deeper into the house.

"Go on in and make yourself a plate," Bethany explained to everyone, standing very near Lillian. "I didn't want to do a whole stodgy thing with hired help serving everyone and all that. Makes me uncomfortable. The house is fancy. I'm not. Hope that doesn't disappoint anyone."

Cindy and Sally looked crestfallen.

"No, I'm much more comfortable this way," Lillian murmured to Bethany.

"Thank you," Bethany murmured back and gestured everyone follow her through deep shadows under a vast arch.

The dining room was long and dark, in mahogany and ebony wood, with two silver suits of armor standing guard on either side of an enormous arched fireplace with a fire lit. The dining room table itself was similarly long, made of smooth, dark wood with enormous carved paws for feet. Place settings were clustered around the end closer to the fire, silver candelabras in elaborate filigree with hefty, shining bases of were lit at the center of a purple velvet table runner.

A spread was laid out on a buffet against the wood-paneled wall and Lillian was glad there were plenty of vegetarian options. After she collected small helpings of different sides on a lovely china plate with a rose-briar rim, she took to the nearest open seat.

"Does anyone mind if we talk business during dinner?" Bethany asked.

The assembled company shook their heads that they didn't mind and began eating.

"We each come to this from our own unique time and place," Bethany began. "While I'm grateful to have my closest collegiate colleagues with me from my graduate writing program," she said, looking around the room with a fond smile before turning to Lillian, "I'm also glad to welcome strangers, but whose work I've appreciated and think can benefit the projects as a whole. Can we go around the table and introduce ourselves?"

Bethany nodded at Lillian to start them off.

"Oh. Hi. I'm Lillian Anders. I'm a historian, tour guide, archivist, a girl out-of-sync with time, you might say…"

"And style," Sally murmured as if she just couldn't help herself. Lillian pointedly ignored her.

"Sally, do introduce yourself," Bethany cut in sharply.

"Hiiii, Sally Winters, influencer, media maven. Along with Cindy here we run a channel that focuses on wild and weird parts of the country. This town *definitely* qualifies. My parents are angel investors in the new Persephone Publications company and thought you all could use some publicity, so we'll be doing a lot of recording and getting clips. Cindy?"

"I'm Cindy Smith, Sally's cousin. We were communications majors at UCLA. We also do color commentary with our travels, focusing on regional differences in fashion, whether a place has or hasn't heard of trends or designers and if that affects their urban legends." She turned to the woman next to her and nodded.

The dark-skinned woman with short-cropped spiral curls, dressed in an elegant blouse smiled. "I'm Anita Wells. I've a background in cultural anthropology and began working on a non-fiction book that became my

26

graduate thesis, so we'll see if fiction or non-fiction comes out of my time here. I appreciate that Bethany has been open to either."

A tall, long-haired dark blonde with a dusting of freckles across rosy cheeks who sat across from Lillian took up the next introduction.

"I'm Serenity," she announced.

"What a beautiful name," Lillian replied, sharing the smile.

"Thanks!" Serenity said proudly. "When you choose your own name and ditch all the assigned stuff, it can become all the more meaningful." She coiled her wrist in a dainty gesture. "Everyone should try it!" With a laugh, she tapped her notebook. "My writing has always been best in essays, prose flash fiction or short-story formats, but I'd like to try longer-form work here. I'm interested in a story about a haunt who manifests their true gender identity for the first time, as a ghost. Presenting, as a spirit, in a way they weren't able to in life, considering a more restrictive past."

"That's great," Bethany exclaimed.

Serenity turned to the Indian woman next to her who was dressed in green silk salwar kameez, the top of the tunic richly embroidered, and smiled. "You're up, Kashvi."

"I'm Kashvi Anand. My graduate thesis was tracing regional variants in Hindu beliefs and practices; how different origin stories for gods and consorts could change from one district to the next and comparing that to folk histories and urban legend in the United States, and what happens when those histories mix. I'd like to bring that concept to the backlist here. I'd like to play with the idea that it isn't an unreliable narrator, it's that it's *multiple* narrators."

Everyone nodded, appreciating the idea.

"As you see," Bethany says proudly, "we've got a range of viewpoints by which we'll be examining the concept of 'women running from houses' and what that may mean in our modern world, from the unique identities and diaspora we bring to the table. But first, sorry, legal stuff."

Bethany handed out a form.

"My lawyers have insisted on this. Because there are a lot of dangers, structurally, to many infamous sites around us, and I know there are adventure seekers among us," Bethany smiled at Cindy and Sally who preened at the attention. "I need to have all of you agree that none of you will trespass into the abandoned mine, whose entrances still exist and are on the Glazier property map, or go anywhere in the mansion that is expressly marked as off-limits. All of this is for safety and structural concerns. Not because the mansion has something its hiding. It just has some holes in the floors in spots. And the mine, well, it's its own gauntlet of dangers. If someone should trespass, the Glazier estate is not liable for injury."

Everyone skimmed the document, fairly straightforward, signed and returned them.

Lillian caught Sally's expression during, as if she was holding back a laugh. The two women were clearly younger than the rest of Bethany's collegiate associates who were likely in their early to mid-thirties like Lillian, but were these two *twelve*? Was everything a joke? If Bethany noticed, she didn't act like it. She was a woman who was confident, smooth and unruffled in everything she did. It was admirable.

"So," she continued, putting the signed papers in a folder. "All of you were given a book to at least start reading from our back catalogue. Who has thoughts?"

Kashvi discussed a book that had a 'haunted foreign object' premise, and it was clear to her that the author hadn't consulted anyone from the cultures concerned, or learned much about the item itself, a Buddhist prayer wheel. She and Bethany traded a weary exchange about the troubling trend of late 19th century and early 20th century orientalism, exoticism and fetishization.

Anita stated that she'd like to write an introduction for the book she read in a reissue, noting that it featured a Black law enforcement officer, and it could serve as a reminder that there were indeed sheriffs of color in the 'old west'.

This led into Serenity discussing what she believed was an allegorical vampire story, and how interested she was in the exploration of power dynamics, gender constructs and psychological manipulation and how she wanted to be less veiled about it in a revised manuscript.

Everyone turned to Lillian. She smiled sheepishly and cleared her throat. No stranger to public speaking giving lectures, presentations and tours at her old job, she was suddenly very nervous as she did want all of these smart women to like and respect her, even the *influencers*.

"To be fair, I haven't finished the book yet. But *The Curse* is a story of star-crossed lovers from different classes, the daughter of a powerful family and a servant to the other powerful family in town. Glancing at the author's note, she thanks local historians so I'm thinking it's taken from or partially inspired by a true story. There's something very real about this couple, I… feel for them." She couldn't share just how overwhelmed she felt by the narrative, she didn't know how to explain that.

As she began discussing the lovers' plot to escape, one of the suits of armor beside the fireplace suddenly moved, dropping its axe down to the floor as if in execution.

Everyone screamed, Lillian perhaps the loudest. Bethany rushed over to the armor, inspecting the elbows. From the floor she picked up a rusty bracket. "The clamp gave way. Impressive timing, though, Lillian."

The breathlessness of the group gave way to laughter. Sally chided Cindy for not having gotten that on camera.

Returning to the table, Bethany gestured to the influencers. "What were your thoughts on the company's old media documents I sent you?"

Cindy began talking about how she could apply a vintage filter and put together a retrospective video, but Lillian stopped listening when a glowing, ethereal form became visible just beyond the arch which led into another part of the house. Her heart began racing and her breath went shallow and strained.

As the entity floated closer, glimmering eyes piercing Lillian, features became clearer. It was unmistakably the striking spirit she'd seen before; the ghost who had appeared in Bethany's video.

Bethany followed Lillian's eyes, turning back to her with a subtle shaking of her head and pursed lips, as if begging Lillian to stay calm. No one else seemed to see the figure, otherwise there would have been more upheaval. Everyone else was focusing on Cindy and Sally's ideas for a short company documentary. If those two could have seen him, they'd *definitely* try to get him on camera.

The ghost kept wafting nearer, his stare eviscerating. Lillian had no idea what to do. What did it want with her? It floated directly behind her chair.

She turned away, the small hairs on the back of her neck standing straight as they froze, a chill racking her body.

The ghost bent down and whispered in Lillian's ear, achingly: "I know you."

"I'm sorry, I'm not feeling very well," Lillian blurted and scrambled to her feet, almost knocking over her chair as it slid through the apparition. "Sorry!" Not knowing what else to do, she ran.

"*Rude*," Sally chastised as Lillian ducked out into the hallway and kept going.

Throwing open the great front doors with an inelegant gasp, Lillian tore from the mansion. Darting back to the carriage house up the gravel lane from the mansion, she kept looking over her shoulder as she ran. The ghost did not follow.

Running inside, she closed the door and leaned against it, breathing heavily. "Way to make first impressions," she murmured ruefully. "Day one and you're certifiable."

Shoulders slumping, she turned into the room.

The fire was lit again.

"What. The. Hell."

The clock on the mantle chimed and Lillian jumped, staring into the mirror above the fireplace. Her face was white as a sheet, terror evident. But then, something shifted. As if she were going out of focus. Her face appeared only partially her own, a superimposed layer; another very similar face was overlaid upon hers. Some odd trick of light, shadow, panic and startled imagination. The lack of sleep was clearly taking its toll.

But Bethany had seen the ghost too. She couldn't be crazy. Who did the spirit think she was? Who was he confusing her for?

Exhausted and overwhelmed, she slumped into one of the armchairs facing the fire—if it was lit, she might as well enjoy the warmth—and picked up the hardcover copy of *The Curse* again. A fresh wave of nerves hit her.

"It is a book you have to read and you're here to do a job," she told herself sternly. "The book can't hurt you, you big baby."

Opening the book, it fell open to the author's note, as if it was begging her to really read it this time, to take it to heart:

Some say truth is stranger than fiction. The unlucky couple in this book were all too real, pulled from the local lore of the town where this book was published. I'd like to honor them in this book, and wish their spirits well, wherever they may be. May the curse that followed them be broken, as no one, and no place, deserves an endless parade of ill luck, misfortunes and early deaths. Here's to true love, may it reign forever.

Lillian picked up her phone and looked up the author's name in conjunction with the book title and her blood went cold as she read:

Martha Green died of a heart attack the day THE CURSE was published, her body found at the base of Glazier Drive, facing one of the old Denny Family mansions the day it caught fire. Locals insist the curse came for her, too.

Lillian threw her phone and the book on the sofa, not wanting to read anything more. Not until she could calm down again. Rushing to her drawstring velvet bag, she fumbled around inside for a smooth stone. Grabbing a large amethyst crystal the size of her palm, she curled up in the armchair again and pressed it to her chest. It had been a gift from one of her co-workers at the museum one week after a series of odd, inexplicable events happened; things had been moved and lights were on when no one was inside. Lillian associated the stone with protection and the weight of it in her hand calmed her.

A wave of sleepiness overtook her, and she tucked into the large chair like a bird in a nest.

The dream was torturously vivid.

He was there. The ghost. But no, this man was alive, vibrant and far more beautiful than his shade portrayed. Lit by the glow of a roaring fire to the side of them, his brown hair was delightfully disheveled, his chestnut eyes sparkled with warmth and care, his cravat was undone, and his shirtsleeves were open. He was holding her tightly in one arm, his other hand reverently caressing the length of her bare arm. A satin gown lay pooled on the floor, only a shift and petticoat remained on her body. Her surroundings looked familiar, but the décor was different.

A clock chimed and she glanced towards the sound. The same brass clock sat on the stone mantel. The carriage house. Alone in the carriage

31

house with a forbidden love…

"Camille," he murmured. "I live for the day we never have to sneak about, lie or subvert again. Soon, I'll wed you and we'll live free, in truth and joy. God, I love you, light of my life. I do hope you know I'd do anything for you."

"I do."

He cupped her face in his hands and kissed her softly, then deeply as she sighed against his lips. She melted into his hold as he guided her back, lowering her so they lay before the fire. He drew back to look down at her. Her heart swelled with boundless emotion.

"I adore you, William," she murmured. "You won't mind that I'll be poor, when I leave all this?"

He smiled, running soft fingers over her brow, across her cheek, grazing her lips. "I don't want your money, my love. I never have. *You're* the treasure. Your kind heart is worth a thousand mansions. I'll provide for you, and we'll make our own choices, taking no orders from anyone. You are your *own* woman and I'd not want it any other way."

"I am yours, though…" she said, fear and anxiety melting away, snaking her arms around him tightly. "I'd not want *that* any other way."

At this, his eyes lit up like a struck flint. He raked a hand down her body, causing her to arch against him with a gasp that woke Lillian in the instant.

Cheeks flushed with desire, skin moist from a sheen of sweat, Lillian pitched forward in the armchair she'd dozed off in and moaned at the stab of pain that arced up her neck from having slept on it wrong. It was daylight and she had no idea how long she'd been asleep.

The fire was out, a pile of ash in its place and she couldn't trust herself to remember if it had been lit before she dozed off or only in the dream. Whirling around, there was no ghost or living being present other than herself. The surroundings were back to their modern renovation, not their Victorian setting.

She knew her friends would have a field day with this if she ever told them.

"First night after a haunting and I have a sexy dream about the ghost in question?" She shook her head. "Way to embody the Gothic heroine…"

Self-deprecatory humor was a must.

But the truth was, the dream had affected her deeply. Her body still felt like she was in his hold, the echo of his touch still making her shiver, his kiss so real, it was more a memory than a dream.

A paper by the door caught her eye. At some point Bethany must have slid a schedule underneath for the next few days. Lillian picked it up and set it by the coffee maker as she made herself a pot. At the top of the schedule Bethany had added a hand-written note:

"I hope you slept ok. Sorry about the ghost? Thanks for not saying anything, though, I'm hoping the others won't freak out. Though we could chalk it up to inspirational atmosphere, ha ha. Is there anything I can do to make you more comfortable? Any ideas, please let me know. I'm out of my depth here in terms of a *real* haunted house, I thought we'd just be writing about them. Thanks for being cool." —Bethany

Lillian quickly texted Bethany that she was ok and apologized for her own rushed exit. She explained that she'd fallen asleep due to insomnia and promised she'd be at the 1pm group pitch-session. Having immediately taken to Bethany, Lillian really didn't want someone she hoped could become a friend thinking she was flighty, unreliable or too sensitive. Everyone had their own relationship to the paranormal. As a goth, it was expected that there was at least an interest in, if not a direct affinity for, the paranormal. But for everyone that was deeply personal; where you drew your own line about what was neat and what was horrific was an entirely subjective boundary.

In the light of day and the verdant green around her, having always been particularly fond of fir trees, the panic in which she'd run from the mansion faded. Looking at the clock, it seemed she had time to explore. There were paths out and around the grounds she was interested in.

The explanation for the dream was simple. It was a product of what she'd been reading, coupled with the fact that the ghost was beautiful. He was an embodiment of all her girlhood fancies. Of course, her mind would embellish the haunting with a scene from a romance novel.

It was the question that haunted her, more than the ghost. Did she remember him? His insistence that he knew or recognized her. Who was Camille?

Changing into a different era in black than her Renaissance dress before, today called for a high-necked Victorian blouse with buttoned-up collar, gauzy black ruffles down the front and subtly puffed sleeves that came to a fitted, v-pointed cuff, the gauze of the ruffles matching the gauzy layers of the flowing skirt. She wound her long hair up in a bun, pinning it with silver hair-sticks tipped with small enamel ravens. She slipped a water bottle and phone into a small bag she could throw over a shoulder. Glancing up at the sky, even though she would be mostly shaded, she put on light layer of 110-proof sunblock and slipped sunglasses into her bag.

Glazier Drive swept up past the carriage house and around a bend. Lillian followed the road for about a hundred yards when she saw an old, rusted metal sign noting *Mine Entrance* and *No Exit*. Around the next curve, the drive came to an abrupt stop and a wooden barricade marked the end of the Drive, beyond which lay endless trees and the mountain continued cresting upward behind it.

An enormous stone arch announced *Glazier Mine. Est. 1865* in bold, carved letters, curved over an entrance that was entirely shuttered. Enormous wooden doors with wrought iron tracery were chained shut and the links had weathered and rusted through the years. *No Trespassing, Keep Out, Danger, Do Not Enter, Mine Shaft* and countless other warning signs were tacked across the entrance and a few graffiti tags danced around the edges.

To the left of the barricaded door curved a long, winding set of stone stairs that climbed upward along a ridge.

Lillian decided to ascend. Taking her time, seeing how she could glimpse bits of Glazier's Gap below in snippets of road, the occasional rooftop, a brightly lit convenience shop and ice cream parlor, a large, partially obscured building that looked like half of it had been eaten by the mountain outcropping behind it.

At the top of the stairs, a clearing opened up. One stone bench and the remnants of two others sat in a grouping, paths diverging into overgrown forest trails that were also barricaded by rusting gates and fallen timbers.

Catching her breath, Lillian moved to sit on the stone bench that remained intact. Unique, deep orange wildflowers grew all around the bench.

"You're pretty," she said to the flowers, touching one of their blossoms gently.

"Jewelweed. Always your favorite wildflower."

Startled by a voice nearby when *no one* had been there a moment ago, she whirled around to behold a man floating a foot off the ground.

Here in the forest, his form phased in and out of pale color and deep shadow. Him again. The ghost who had bent close to her ear in the mansion. The beautiful man she'd been kissing in her dream when he'd been solid rather than shade. Her cheeks went immediately red. He stared at her curiously, knowingly.

"What do you mean my favorite wildflower?" Lillian snapped. "You don't know anything about me! You're not even real. You're just a figment of… imagination. I must be having a… profound mental schism."

"No, you're not. You'll learn all manner of wondrous things happen in this town. Beautiful and terrible. I'm glad you can see me. The others who I'd hoped would be our second chance couldn't."

"Couldn't what?"

"See me, let alone remember. Do you?" he asked hopefully.

"That again?" Lillian folded her arms, uncomfortable. "Only that you were the ghost in Bethany's screen! And you made me seem like a lunatic after dinner when you appeared again." Lillian bit her tongue so as to *not* mention the dream. It was a dream. Not a memory. A dream.

He looked crestfallen. "Is that all?"

"Am I supposed to know something more?"

He offered a slight, mournful smile. "I hope you will."

"What's that supposed to *mean*? Don't be so cryptic."

He floated a little closer. "If it's meant to be, you'll know. I don't want to convince you if you don't, truly, want to know. Perhaps you don't want to remember. You are still your own woman and I want you always to make your own choices." There was such a gentle loveliness about him, a quality that rose above the deep sadness in his eyes. His words were similar to what had been said in her dream. How could she have intuited that?

She found herself wanting to remember something, wanting to help him, somehow. The passionate scenes from her dream flashed before her and she had to close her eyes and not look at him. She couldn't tell him that.

"What is it?" he asked. "I used to have no secrets with Camille."

Lillian kept her arms folded so he wouldn't see her trembling. "Who is Camille? I don't know any Camille."

"The woman I love," he responded softly, his form brightening as he said it.

An enormous flock of starlings burst from a tree overhead, startling Lillian.

The ghost studied the birds for a long moment. "Be careful. Any time I've ever seen a murmuration that large, someone dies. If you find precious things, hold them close. They'll protect you. Simple things. Anything you love. And try to remember. Because *if* the memories are in you, you might feel more at ease by letting them out…"

Uneasily, Lillian backed away. "Ok…" The mention of someone dying was enough to truly scare her. "I have to go." Gathering her skirts, she turned and began descending the long stone stairs as quickly as she safely could.

Wait. He hadn't said *Camille* before today. How did her dream last night know it was Camille he was looking for?

She didn't have time to think about this further before the warning of the blackbirds became clear.

As Lillian arrived at the bottom of the stairs, she heard two terrible screams. Then a disgusting, heavy thud as if something landed from high above.

Out from under the closed mine door, the bottom of a mine shaft, blood began flowing in dreadful rivulets, rushing towards Lillian. A crimson stream spreading out on the sloping stone drive.

With a gasping cry, Lillian ran back down Glazier Drive towards the mansion, pulling her phone out and calling 911, breathlessly explaining that she heard a scream and saw blood coming out from under the mine entrance, even though it remained closed. There had to be some other way in. The operator told her to remain on the line.

Outside the Glazier mansion, shaded by the portico, Serenity was looking at her phone and then at Lillian in horror. Bethany was sitting, looking shell-shocked on the bench by the door.

"I heard a scream, there was blood…" Lillian gestured weakly back up the hill. "I'm on hold with 911 dispatch."

Shaking, Serenity held out her phone. A video began playing the scene: a shaky video of a woman holding a flashlight along a metal rail in a hollowed-out stone tunnel.

"C-Cindy. And Sally… They were livestreaming," Serenity explained. "Going into the mine. Watch."

"And here we are at the abandoned mine shaft, from this ledge we don't know how far down it goes," Cindy explained. "In the 19th century, *many* deaths were reported here."

Then Cindy flailed, screamed, and fell out of frame as Sally shrieked. The terrible thud. Lillian turned and vomited in a holly bush by the foot of the portico.

"Someone… something pushed Cindy." Serenity said, ignoring Lillian getting sick, her voice rising in panic. "But Sally was filming. Nothing was there. *No one* was there!"

She was right. No one had been there. Lillian turned back to the video. Like being unable to keep from craning your neck towards a car wreck.

The video continued with Sally screaming and running, the camera now just a bouncing blur against Sally's flashlight and then a thud and skidding sound. The video stopped. Serenity, dazed, put her phone in the pocket of her skirt and turned towards Bethany, who sat staring blankly forward.

"Are you still there, Miss Anders?" the operator prompted.

"Yes. I'm at the Glazier mansion. There might be someone still in the mine. On an upper ledge."

"Were you in the mine with the victim?"

"No, I was outside. The doors on my side were still shut. They… two people livestreamed going in. Then the video just cut out. We haven't seen either woman come out. Cindy… definitely fell on the video." Lillian was shaking so hard her voice was jumping and hitching. "Maybe Sally fell on the path above? I don't know where any other entrance is to get to her, though, I only know the closed gate where I heard the fall."

"EMTs are two minutes out. Keep your phone with you, you'll likely need to make a statement."

"Ok…"

The operator hung up.

An ambulance came roaring up the drive, a police car behind it, behind that, a fire truck. Serenity went to sit silently with Bethany. Lillian, not knowing what to do, or who to be with, followed the vehicles.

The fire team was already hard at work cutting the chains and the huge wooden and metal bolts that had kept the old entrance secured and barricaded. When the doors swung open with a terrible, wrenching roar, Lillian winced. Glimpsing part of a bloody mess as the team went in to set up a scene around the body, she had to turn away, bile rising in her throat again. She'd never get that sound out of her mind; the sound of a falling body hitting bottom.

Rescuers working on a higher level within the mine's structure managed to lower an unconscious Sally down to the clearing level on an orange, padded stretcher and wheel her into the ambulance before it roared away.

Lillian's eye was drawn to a floating figure on the stairs, looking on in horror. Terrified all over again, she wondered if the ghost had something to do with it.

Chapter Four

A YOUNG, DARK-HAIRED, OLIVE-SKINNED officer approached Lillian, dressed in a simple dark suit, his badge on his belt. He asked if she was the one to call it in. Lillian nodded and explained everything that happened. The detective put it all down in a notebook, along with her contact information.

"What a welcome to Glazier's Gap," the officer said ruefully. "I promise it's not all this bad."

"Hope not," Lillian replied nervously. "I'm… can I go back to the mansion?" She couldn't do anything to help here but perhaps she could help Bethany somehow.

"Yes, if anyone else has other questions, we'll look for you there."

Lillian thought to mention that Bethany had warned them, and about their signed forms, but thought better of it. If she was defensive on the retreat's behalf, it might look more suspicious. Ignoring the warning, Cindy and Sally foolishly did a stunt that cost a life. Simple as that. Lillian still felt terrible, though, and she was sure Bethany would feel far worse.

When Lillian returned, Bethany rose and ran over to her. It was clear she'd been crying. "Is… did…"

"Sally was rushed off in the ambulance, so there's hope there," Lillian explained. "I… I wasn't inside the mine to see anything about Cindy but… it didn't look good. I made a statement with one of the detectives, they'll likely question all of us. I told them I was coming back here. Can I… do anything? Can I help, somehow?"

"I don't know what to tell you," Bethany murmured. "Are you someone who likes to work when something bad happens, or--"

"Yes. Can I get started cataloguing the items in the Archive?"

Bethany nodded, seeming as glad to think of something else as Lillian was. As they went inside, Lillian asked. "Where is everyone else?"

"In their rooms. I told Anita and Kashvi what happened, they'd been at lunch. Everyone is free to stay here or go, our retreat is now… officially off the rails. So, it's anyone's guess what folks will do. I just… wanted everyone to be comfortable, excited, *safe*--"

"This had nothing to do with you, none of this is your fault," Lillian reassured.

"I know. I just wish it hadn't happened."

"Me too. But you did your due diligence."

Bethany walked her through the entrance foyer and through a disorienting, darkened set of rooms Lillian wasn't sure she'd get the hang of navigating again.

"It was my nightmare," Bethany said mordantly, "that something like this would happen. I just hope nothing else goes wrong. I don't blame anyone for leaving. You either."

They were walking through a dimly lit room full of taxidermized animals that very much unsettled Lillian.

"I've… got nowhere else to go. I hadn't told you this before, but I'd unexpectedly lost my job the day we first talked. My position was being sourced out to a recording. So being able to work here is a real help." Lillian glanced around nervously. An alligator's jaws were open very near her arm. "But I won't mind getting out of the dead critter room."

"Right. Sorry."

"It may seem like an antithetical thing for a goth not to like taxidermy but, you know, vegetarian and all. Dead animals just make me sad."

"Well, here we are." Bethany gestured her into the next hallway, towards an elaborately carved door and opened it with a long, old key.

The Archive was a very large, very strange room.

The interior was done as a Victorian revival, but this too in a 1970s version, where all the color choices were profoundly garish and jarring.

"It's weird in here, I know. *I'm* haunted by the colors," Bethany said with disdain.

Lillian chuckled. "You said it, not me."

"In these glass bookcases are every book the publisher once published." Bethany gestured to a wall of glass cabinets stacked with paper, newspaper clippings and boxes. "This, from what I can gather, all has to do with the town and the publishing company, some of it research material for some of the books, some of it marked, some not, none of it sorted in any kind of order that I can figure."

"Where would you like me to start?"

"Maybe here," Bethany said quietly, pointing through the glass of a nearby cabinet to a big box marked: THE CURSE – RESEARCH MATERIALS. "I realize that in every horror film, this is the box you're not supposed to touch, but…"

"It's the one I'd be curious enough about to open anyway. Unable to help myself. I'll be Pandora to a lot of boxes here, I've a feeling. But hey." Lillian shrugged. "Perhaps I can recover some hope left inside."

Bethany smiled. "That's a lovely thought. Thank you, Lillian. I'm so glad Keri introduced us."

"Me too."

"Will you be all right if I leave you? I'm… going to have to talk to my lawyers."

"I'll be fine."

"I'll be in the parlor making calls, don't hesitate to come in if you need anything."

"Vice versa."

Bethany lingered a moment before reaching out and hugging Lillian briefly.

Returning the hug, Lillian added, "I guess we just take all of these weird, difficult things one moment at a time, huh?"

41

Withdrawing, wiping her eyes, Bethany nodded. "Yeah. We do. Sorry about that," she said, embarrassed. "I'm usually the strong one."

"Strong ones need hugs too."

Bethany allowed a half-smile and walked away. Watching her go a moment, Lillian thought about how she had never been the strong one, not really, so it was nice to step up to that plate. No one would envy the position Bethany was put in, as the death would cast a terrible light on anything she wanted to do with the company, even though none of it was her fault. Everyone else here knew Bethany and knew that strength above all else. Sometimes it took someone from the outside seeing in to unlock something needed.

She turned to the archive room, squaring her shoulders, trying to live into a newfound strength. "What needs unlocking in here?"

Refusing to think about anything but work, she opened the box marked THE CURSE.

There were tons of notes, some written on bar napkins labeled The Blue Taper with a silver candlestick logo and a blue candle. Some of these were the first lines of text of the book, others were notes about people, urban legends, things locals shared. It would seem Martha Green wasn't a local, she'd been a New York writer hired to write the book and spent a year here doing so.

Taking the box to a gaudy, mauve-painted desk all the way across the room, she wiped the dust off a wing-backed chair, turned on an imitation Tiffany glass dragonfly lamp done in obnoxious colors, and took a seat as she continued sorting.

There was an author photo inside, one that hadn't been included in the electronic edition Bethany had sent her, nor had it made it onto the dustcover of the original book.

Lillian had to sit back a moment, holding the black and white photo in her hand, unsettled by the fact that there was a distinct resemblance between her and Martha Green.

"That's… weird," she said aloud, as if that might make uncanny things seem less spooky.

A yellowed newspaper article in a plastic sheet, taken from the Glazier

Gazette, dated 1888 discussed a family rivalry between the Glazier and Denny family. The pre-existing animosity between the prominent families had intensified after a Denny family member, a manager who had been giving a tour to manufacturing firms, died in the mine owned by the Glaziers. It was said he had fallen from a great height as if he'd been pushed, but witnesses said no one was within an arm's length of him to do so.

"Can the past try... *not* to repeat itself right now?" she said to the paper.

This had been what she'd always done when strange things happened in the museum when she was alone there. She'd talk to the room, to the situation, and in doing so, her calling it out would make whatever odd thing it was seem absurd. It was the only way she kept herself calm and maintained perspective. In one case, a historic photograph she'd placed inside a display cabinet had been turned upside down the next day. After she made a verbal admonishment, when she turned back, it was right side up again. She wished it could work for things like.... Bringing someone back to life. She hadn't liked Cindy or Sally, but it hadn't meant she wanted either of them hurt or dead.

Another clipping from earlier in 1888, still from the same local paper, was an excerpt from a gossip column, noting that one of the Denny daughters was refusing to marry a prominent English baronet, going on to perpetuate a rumor that she was in love with someone well below her wealthy class. The columnist seemed to delight in this, and Lillian wondered if some of the high society in the town liked stoking the rivalry themselves. Everyone likely had an angle.

At the bottom of the box was something wrapped in tissue paper. Carefully unfolding it, she pulled out an old daguerreotype of a man and a woman, hand in hand.

Lillian's heart leapt to her throat. The man pictured was, unmistakably, the ghost. The woman looked *very* much like Lillian. The names William Hart and Camille Denny were written in light pencil script. The names in her dream. Names she hadn't known yet. And there had been that moment in the mirror, when there was another face, only just slightly different from her own--

"You found it," murmured a voice by her ear as a cold chill spread over her body.

Crying out as she jumped, the photo went spinning over the dusty desk and she whirled to behold the ghost floating by her side.

"What's going on, what is all this?" Lillian squeaked out.

"Nothing has come back to you?"

"What? You… think I'm this woman in this photo?"

"At least *some* part of Camille's spirit chose you. Fates aligning to bring you here, the resemblance just part of the magic." The spirit's voice was so gentle, so full of care, she felt like she should be terrified, but his regard for her made it very hard to know what to think. He pressed on, with an earnest and uncomfortable truth. "Haven't you always felt you were looking for something? Haven't you always felt a bit lost?"

Lillian swallowed hard and didn't answer. He was right, but she didn't dare embolden him.

But glancing at him, she couldn't help but remember her dream and her cheeks flushed in a telling wave of heat. His presence affected her. Overwhelmed her. Made her dizzy. Hungry, in a way she feared and desired in equal measure. But the sobering events of the day pressed in.

Scared about the answer, she knew she wouldn't stop thinking about it unless she screwed up her courage. Closing her eyes, she blurted, "Where were you when Cindy fell? You were at the top of that crest--"

"It wasn't me. I promise you."

"There was footage. *Something* pushed her but nothing could be seen on the video--"

"And you see me on film, do you not? You saw me in Bethany's device, before you even came here?"

Lillian nodded.

"I can't touch anyone," he added sadly, coming close. Lillian breathed in sharply as he tried to wrap his arm around her and draw her to him. His arm passed through, causing Lillian to shudder violently. "I certainly can't push anyone. It was, unfortunately, the curse that took her. Things sometimes… repeat, here, in this town."

"A curse, the curse, like in the book?"

"Yes, more or less. I don't, to tell you the truth, know entirely how it works, but because of the tragedy that befell Camille--" he gestured to the daguerreotype, "-and I... Ever since, if someone has malevolent or even duplicitous intent while on Glazier property, it makes them vulnerable to the curse. Maiming or death. It's happened a couple of times before, but since no-one has been living in the mansion for some time, nor running the publishing company, it's just been thought coincidence. But, alas, it isn't."

"What tragedy? Be specific."

"Keep reading, you'll find all our sad details, more or less. When you do, perhaps whatever of her spirit might live on in you will... wake up. I want to encourage you, but ultimately, you have to find her yourself."

She had to look away from him; his presence was too mesmerizing. "What do you think will stop the curse?"

"I don't know. No matter what happened, I don't want others to be hurt or killed because of anything to do with me. I don't know who *set* the curse after my death."

"Can I help? I don't like the idea of senseless suffering either."

"You're helping by being here. There are things you can touch and affect. Keep searching. If you can find who set the curse, maybe we can find out how to undo it so no one else gets hurt on our—my—account. There's only so much we memories can do."

"Memories? You're not a ghost?"

"Not exactly. We echoes speak with those who can hear us and come to those who we are connected to, in dreams."

Lillian gulped. "In dreams?" Her already flushed face went impossibly redder, her pulse throbbing at her temples. The ghost drew closer.

"Yes. In dreams." He bent towards her, his voice a sweet, cool breeze against her lips. "Did you dream of me?"

Feeling faint, all she wanted to do was let him touch her; an icy, spectral caress to ease the fever that had been coming over her. The past felt close, as if she could open up any door in this entire mansion and it would be the 1880s and everything might fall into place...

Just as the cool trace of his hands reached out and cupped her face in an exquisite murmur of a touch, the door opened. She jumped up, whirling to the open door, unsteady on her feet.

"Miss, who are you talking to?" It was the officer from before.

"I'm…" She turned back to William only to find he was gone. "Talking to myself."

Chapter Five

A FEW MORE QUESTIONS ANSWERED about the timeline of events, the detective was on his way again, and Lillian passed through a dim sequence of strange rooms, once accidentally turning the wrong way and down a darkened hallway full of empty landscape art and forlorn-looking statues. Even inanimate objects here seemed to carry emotional weight. Continually glancing over her shoulder as she tried to find her way to the front of the house, the ghost had not returned to speak with nor guide her.

Finally winding her way back to the entrance foyer, the detective and his partner were just leaving out the front door. Joining Bethany in the far brighter parlor room, Lillian saw that Serenity, Kashvi and Anita had clustered inside too, each lost in thought, a computer or a device. There was a coffee pot on a hutch with some small sandwiches, and Lillian realized she really needed to eat something, even if the day's events had put off any appetite.

"Hey, friends, so now that the rest of us are here," Bethany began quietly. Lillian sat with her coffee and snack. "The Smiths, the angel investors, have, unsurprisingly, pulled funding. I know none of you can afford to stay on without pay or offset, so I'll change flights and send everyone back at any point they want. Lillian is staying on to help me organize the archive, and the company does have administrative assets saved up to ensure payment. If there's any project you want to finish while here, be my guest, but I have no expectations. When I can regroup some, we can try this again in less jarring circumstances."

Bethany's friends discussed their various projects and timelines, Anita and Serenity both decided they'd use a week to finish up a paper and a script they'd been behind on. Kashvi would take the flight home but reassured her friend that she would come back any time the writer's retreat officially resumed.

"For my part," Lillian said. "I'll take as much work in the Archive as your budget allows."

Bethany nodded. "I can only do part-time while I'm scrambling, but I suggest picking up additional hours at the local historical society. It's located in the primary Denny family mansion down the hill and across Main. They just consolidated family papers and records from two other Denny mansions and their director told me to send someone her way if I found any good candidates."

"Good, I'll check in with them tomorrow, thank you," Lillian stated. "I'm going to that shop on Main to pick up a few things for the carriage house, does anyone need anything?"

No one volunteered anything, so Lillian strode off purposefully down the lane and took in her tree-lined surroundings. At the base of Glazier Drive, the dark closeness of the Douglas firs gave way to the burning gold of tall, elegant Aspen trees in early fall, bright yellow leaves against pale white trunks with black notches. It was so dramatically pretty here.

Across Main Street, a decorative wrought-iron arch with an old Gaslamp lantern curved over a slate stone drive. The drive arced up to a grey stone castle of a building with a black slate mansard roof. Burgundy detailing lined prominent windows and the arched front door, giving the eyes and mouth of the house a red-rimmed look. Her eyes fixed on the uppermost turret, and the rooftop widows' walk around it. Something about it made her feel instantly queasy.

The building unsettled Lillian in a way the Glazier mansion did not, but she couldn't tell if that's because the ghosts of Camille and William's love,

48

and their fates, were urging her on somehow, informing how she looked at this world.

She had to set aside any further feeling about the house as she needed to enquire about employment within, uneasy vibe or no. It was a historic house like any other. Every old house had a weight of history to it, a host of joys and misfortunes. Houses, like people, had layers of complications and patches over cracks and flaws that grew in number every year. One had to make peace with haphazard repairs.

Turning away from the mansion, she was unwilling to let it unnerve her further.

The town was quiet mid-day, not much traffic. She passed a gabled wooden building with large metal letters declaring ANTIQUES, but the shop was closed. In the windows sat beautiful, old, Victorian things: frames, crystal goblets, silver trays and wooden furnishings. Lillian felt the lure, objects calling out to her like long-lost friends; a dangerous siren call when she was on a tight budget.

The liveliest spot in town at the moment seemed to be the Blue Taper bar. The bar sat to the side of the abandoned ski resort that loomed above it about half a mile from Glazier Drive. Mid-century minimalist architecture jutted out garishly from the rockslide that had obliterated half of the structure that Lillian felt was surely haunted.

A ski lift went up the side of the slope and even though everything around the lift chairs was overgrown and the mechanisms were likely long ago shut down, she could have sworn they moved out of the corner of her eye. A sign for a *new* ski resort, with an arrow noting its location ".5 miles away," stood at the foot of the old lifts. The sign seemed as old as the abandoned resort and the picture on it showed a Victorian-looking lodge at the crest of a hill. Yet another quirk of the town; opening a 'new' resort that looked older than the one it had lost.

The small shack of a convenience store aptly named *The Shack* didn't have a large selection but there was enough to get her started with a few staples.

Walking back with a bag on her arm, the light seemed at such a different angle than when she'd started out. She supposed it was the difficulty of being nestled between two dramatic rises one on each side; that bright light was fleeting and far more often than not, the town existed in shadow.

As she crossed in front of the historical society again, she could have sworn she heard a fight in the upstairs floors. A woman was screaming, crying and begging. A deep voice was shouting and decrying her; a vicious admonishment of disloyalty bellowing over her tears.

But there were no lights on in the mansion. A gust of wind swept through, whisking the sound away again as if it were a dead leaf tumbling into the underbrush.

A place of deep shade and dramatic echoes, Lillian leaned into the romanticism a location like this could offer. If she could hold these buildings in that very gothic light, embracing the idea that the past was watching with care to share its secrets with her, it was a more palatable notion than being unnerved by spectral voyeurism from another era.

Chapter Six

RETURNING TO THE CARRIAGE HOUSE, Lillian glanced first at the fireplace. It was out. Just a pile of grey ash. She made a fresh pot of coffee, put logs on the fire from a small stack of firewood to the side of the great hearth, and interspersed the open stack with tinder from a large copper trunk on the opposite side of the fireplace, striking a long match from a filigree box on the mantel and tending the base until the logs caught.

Sitting down in the armchair closest to the fire with a steaming mug, she picked up the hardcover edition of *The Curse* and continued reading, every page like a discomfiting, too-personal journal entry from a diary she'd never written.

As she read, she couldn't help but see it unfolding as if she were thrust into a film, immersive in a way that defied her mind's eye and resembled resurfaced memories instead.

The lovers, Caroline and Wesley are entwined in a lover's embrace in his quarters.

Lillian noted with discomfort that his quarters were within a carriage house. Nervously, Lillian looked up and around her, as if at any time her modern renovation could have reverted to its Victorian self.

Lillian had to close her eyes a moment after Caroline was ripped from

Wesley's arms by a threatening father and then imprisoned by her family in a tower on their property. She was treated like a criminal just for having the audacity not to care that the man she loved had less money than she. One of Lillian's hands curled into a fist as she read.

Caroline soon grows very ill, her symptoms likely tuberculosis, exacerbated by poor conditions. Relatives plead with her to agree to marry a wealthy British aristocrat so the family can have a title. She refuses to marry—and to then be forced to be intimate with—a man she does not love.

Wesley has made it a habit to always look up to the tower and bid her goodnight before returning to his side of the hill that separates them, even if she can't see or hear him at her heights.

The desolation in the narrative was almost unbearable, two very dear hearts in absolute tatters, not knowing how to overcome the forces that were beyond their capacity or power to change.

Feeling nauseous, Lillian's eyes kept filling with tears. Because of the ghost's insistence on her remembering a past like this one, she couldn't trust that she wasn't psychosomatically creating a connection and a false memory the more she read. How could she trust reality?

Managing to pick the lock of her prison one night, Caroline wanders out onto the slick, icy parapets, trying to find a way to climb down and escape. But instead of stumbling to freedom, she falls to her death.

Lillian gasped, thinking of the tower of the Denny mansion and how queasy it had made her. She continued reading even though her body had broken out into a cold sweat.

Wesley is, of course, the one who finds Caroline's body when he comes to bid her his lonely goodnight. He calls for help but once discovered, he is taken into custody as her murder suspect. That night, in the jail cell, all hope lost, he dies of a broken heart.

As Caroline is laid in a fine tomb and Wesley in a pauper's plot, a witch high on a hill curses the family who brought this upon the young lovers. The witch cries out into the night:

"To any who would deny true love and soul mates, and instead valorize status and wealth, to thee, I say, fall from a great height. And keep falling. All will fall who do not lift up noble, gentler hearts so that they may be let

to live free."

The last lines of the book read like a warning, as if it should have been posted, carved in the rock over the Keep Out signs at the entrance to the mine:

> *And the curse did come collect in that town. One by one, nearly all those who tried to break the girl were felled themselves by mysterious illness. Beware great greed and falling from great heights. Beware the ghosts made from broken hearts.*

Lillian turned the last page to find an editor's note and another newspaper clipping in a plastic sleeve, slipped beneath the back fold of the dust jacket.

The editor's addendum noted what Lillian had seen online: that the author died of a heart attack the day the book was released, coinciding with a fire in a local mansion used as inspiration for the book. There was no further commentary in the note, as if you were meant to draw your own conclusions.

Slipping the old newspaper article out from plastic, she noted it was a copy of a 19th century paper. The Glazier Gazette described the tragic, falling death of the "reclusive Camille Denny" and went on to account that the man who found her, William Hart, died in police custody in a manner a doctor could not fathom. But those who knew the gossip of the town insisted that the young man died of a broken heart.

Slowly, Lillian put the book down, reached a trembling hand for a sip of coffee, and tried to stand up, shakily.

Glancing at herself in the mirror above the mantel, she recoiled.

"You..." she said to her reflection; a woman who looked *so* very much like her, in a 19th century gown. The gown Camille Denny had been pictured in with William at her side, in a daguerreotype that must have been taken surreptitiously by a sympathetic Glazier staff or family member, was reflected on her body.

Camille stared back at her from the glass.

"It didn't happen exactly like in that book," the woman said in Lillian's reflection; a sadder, wearier version of Lillian's voice. "But the woman imprisoned in a turret room and falling to her death, and her love dying of a broken heart? That was, unfortunately true. I tried to get the author to remember. To feel me. Us. But she just couldn't. Her heart wasn't strong enough. But now *you're* here. For our second chance. Will you let me in, finally? Will you, now that you know I am with you, within you… will you let us remember?"

Lillian squeezed her eyes shut. "No. I'm sorry. You must be mistaken. I am myself. I'm not anyone else. I may be delusional, but I am myself." When she opened her eyes again, her reflection was still Camille, staring back at her knowingly.

"Yes, you are yourself, in the end. But I, here, am the memory and the passion that William and I shared. His manifestation is the same; the ghost of our lost love, bound to this town we were never able to escape. My spirit is wrapped up in you. Here, I'm brought out. I'm summoned. This town does that. It creates ghosts out of everyone's hopes and dreams. Or terrors. Some live oblivious and have no idea what's driving them, others know and become obsessed with what they can't grasp. I just want for all of us… to be free. Just… keep your heart open and see what happens. See if William will come here, a new man, just as you've come here, a new woman? Can you do that? Live in hope with me?"

"I *don't* understand." Lillian closed her eyes again, tears streaming down her face. "This is terrifying, not knowing what to do or *who* I am…"

"Let it all be. Let us all *be*. Can you do that?" The murmur of a past faded.

When she opened her eyes again finally, she saw just herself; an overwhelmed, pale face in a black dress. She debated about where to go and what to do.

Grabbing her phone, she refilled her coffee and prayed Keri would pick up.

"Hi, how's it going? Are you ok? Bethany texted me about what happened in the mine. I'm so sorry. She said you had to be the one who called it in."

"Yeah, it was… terrible. But it isn't the only strange thing that's gone on here. There's… so much. I don't even know how to begin."

"You've seen that ghost again, haven't you?"

"How'd you know?"

"Just a feeling. That ghost... it was like he knew you."

"Yes... And he wants me to remember a past life. A woman who looks just like me. The events of the book I was reading... really happened. I don't know what to do. I don't know what is the past coming to call, I don't know what my mind is making up... I don't know if I'm thrilled or scared, if I should stay or leave...."

"Do what your heart tells you to do," Keri offered. "Do what feels good."

"I don't know if I know my own mind or my heart."

"You know what feels safe, even if a little risky, you know the line. The minute you truly don't feel safe there, get out, go one town over, put a hotel room night on a credit card and rethink everything from there."

"I... I know this is going to sound even crazier but..." Lillian explained the reflection and how she spoke with her. "And damn if there isn't this hope within me, this strong, burning fire that was lit in me the moment Camille said it. That someone will come to make it all make sense."

"Well, then maybe give that a chance. Knowing you, you'll always wonder if you don't give the events there a little time to sort out their meaning."

"Yes. You're right. Thank you."

"Keep me posted. I got you into this, I gotta make sure you are good with it."

"Tons of love."

There was an edge of excitement that was barely outpacing her apprehension and so she printed out a resume from the small workstation in the bedroom and planned to drop it at the historical society the next day.

She then created a list of links to information on temperature and humidity control equipment that special collections libraries used for their documents and storage and sent that to Bethany. As she sent it, she heard a ding on someone's phone. A moment later, there was a knock at her door.

"Lillian, it's Bethany, we're going down to get ice cream because we've freaked ourselves out in the house. Want to come?"

"Be right there!" Lillian refreshed her eyeliner, decided she would go the extra mile and put on black lipstick just so finishing touches of goth would be unmistakable, touched up her hair and swept out the door. Serenity and Bethany were dressed in cute dresses, Anita in jeans and a blouse. Bethany led the way down Glazier Drive and the rest followed.

"So, do I *dare* ask what happened in the house to freak you out?" Lillian asked the group. Perhaps the others saw the ghost that Bethany and Lillian had seen.

"*Someone*," Anita eyed Serenity warily, "found a Ouija board--"

"Oh no," Lillian held her hands up. "That's a non-starter. Those things are always bad news."

"That's what *I* said!" Anita turned to Serenity with a wagging finger, "When the *goth* says that's a no-no, it's a *no-no*, Serenity!"

"In my defense, I was just curious," Serenity said earnestly. "The house is weird but it's a *good* kind of weird; I just wanted to see if the house had anything to say about everything that happened."

"You don't get to *pick* what comes through, though," Anita insisted. "That's the problem with those things, it's an imprecise doorway, and without proper ceremony, stuff that just wants to mess with people will come through. You can't summon a house to talk with you. All you can do is interpret the energy of the house. It's not a spirit in the same way."

Serenity clicked acrylic nails together and made a face at Anita, turning to explain the rest to Lillian. "Well, the planchette started moving of its own accord, no one was touching it, so I threw it against the wall and that was that."

Bethany shook herself, as if trying to free herself from chills. "It was *freaky*."

"And you put it away…" Lillian prompted.

"And I put it away," Serenity finished.

When they paused a moment, facing the historical society, Lillian glanced up at the façade of the house, noting something eerily curious. On the second floor, even though there had clearly been painting and restoration involved, there was still fire damage that evidently could not be removed from the wide, thick stone detailing around the windows. Two sets of markings, unmistakably like handprints but with long, claw-like digits, marked the exterior of the sill, as if something monstrous had pushed itself out from the window, leaving sooty prints behind. Lillian shuddered again as they kept walking.

"Cold chill?" Anita asked.

"Yeah."

"The Dennys will do that to you," Bethany muttered. Lillian eyed her. "I'm sorry. I should be setting a better example than my ancestors and I shouldn't slander the 'rival' family. All that's dead and gone now."

"They... don't sound like they were nice, though."

"I'm sure they were nice to some people, just not my family, particularly. And definitely not to my mother. They made a few pointed comments about 'Orientals' that she countered with grace, but we were all really startled by the vitriol. I'm glad the descendants aren't in town often. They're mostly scattered now."

"They weren't nice to their own, either," Lillian said, gesturing back to the house that was now behind them. "They wouldn't let Camille Denny marry the man she loved, so they imprisoned her in the tower instead. She fell from it and died."

"That's terrible," Serenity murmured.

"It's what *The Curse* is based on, I learned," Lillian stated. "And I'm sure I'll learn more working for the historical society, if they'll take me."

"I know Ms. Guidano really needs the help. She'll be lucky to have you," Bethany assured. "Just promise me you won't work there more than in our archives. I really need the help too!"

"I don't know how long I'll be able to be in that house without it... creeping me out too much. Like Serenity said, your mansion is a good kind of weird. *That* one--"

"Well, it is cursed," Bethany finished. Lillian couldn't argue.

A silence descended, as if the reality of Cindy's recent death crowded in again, a sudden punch to their guts.

The ice cream parlor, lit brightly with neon and surrounded by picnic tables that had most of their formerly pastel paint worn off, was a snapshot of the 1950s, A&W Root Beer floats and all. They sat at the furthest outside table, tucked under a broad, golden Aspen, the distance a respite from the raucous overnight-camp kids in matching shirts wreaking havoc with makeshift slingshots.

"I would have taken everyone to The Blue Taper because what we *really* need is a *drink* but it's karaoke night and I'm sorry, there's just only so much off-key singing my nerves can take," Bethany said. "Soon, though. First round's on me."

"Only after I get my requisite word-count in," Serenity qualified, sweeping a long lock of hair behind her shoulder before returning to her cup of sorbet. "I haven't given up on trying to make this time productive."

"Do you believe in past lives?" Lillian asked the group, blurting it out as if she'd been holding it in forever.

Serenity shrugged. "I'm not sure."

Anita thought a moment. "I think I'm informed by my ancestors, by their love, by what they'd want for me, but I don't know that I believe we're recycled from the past."

"I'm not sure that I believe in past lives so much as I believe that the past can somehow be simultaneous," Bethany mused. "I'm disoriented often, as if things shift just slightly when I'm not looking."

"There is something really unique about this place," Anita said. "Didn't you say, Bethany, that the Ute tribe didn't want anything to do with this area on account of it having weird energy?"

Bethany nodded. "The tribe basically said 'have at it' to settlers when they first were exploring the area. Because of it, that meant no conflict or violence over stolen land happened here, thankfully. But there's something to the tribe's avoidance. The area has had its fair share of disasters. I'm not sure the mine was ever safe, then there was the big avalanche and landslide that took out the resort, there have been tons of fires, economic instability regarding the local silver manufacturer, and then there's time. *Time* is just funny." Bethany turned to Lillian. "Sorry we're no help about past lives. What do you believe, though?"

Lillian fiddled with her collar nervously. "I've always believed in them. Just... a little bit more. Here."

"My friend Abby is really into past lives, and she says certain places will trigger memories." Anita looked around them, one tall slope across the street to the one behind them, and the sweep of her eyes made Lillian consider that the land seemed poised and ready to swallow them all up. "Have you had that experience here? Memories, coming back?"

Bethany looked away, as if bracing for a discussion about the ghost.

"Yes? I think?" Lillian said cautiously, pointedly avoiding any mention of William. "But it was likely just a dream. But it was… someone I loved and lost. And I can't quite shake it." The women nodded, thoughtful. But no one had an answer. "Sure, will enjoy that drink…" Lillian added in a murmur.

"The convenience store," Bethany pointed to the neon Coors sign hanging in the window of The Shack, "has a *woefully* small selection of alcohol, which is a damn shame because Colorado has the best craft beers in the nation, but it's better than nothing."

After procuring supplies from The Shack, the women returned to their respective abodes, bidding one another good night and promising not to let anything freak them out any further.

Back in the carriage house, Lillian drank a stout quickly, hoping it could ease her into a dreamless sleep. No such luck.

She dreamt she was in a cold, dark room where she couldn't stop shaking or coughing. Dimly, she could make out a candlestick near her, with a box of matches. Striking the match and lighting the candle, she turned and found herself joining a procession of people all in black.

Everyone was dressed in period clothes of the late 19th century—1880s, by the look of the style of skirts. They were processing up to a lacquered wooden coffin draped in black crepe. She didn't want to look down into the casket, dreading what she'd see.

Sure enough, it was her. Camille. Their faces so alike.

But this one, lifeless in the coffin. Dressed in a lovely blue gown that heightened the blue of her dead lips. Her dead eyes opened and stared back at Lillian, who tried to recoil but who was frozen in place.

"Thank you for coming, Lillian," the corpse murmured. "We've been waiting for you."

Chapter Seven

STANDING BEFORE THE BURGUNDY DOOR of the Glazier's Gap Historical Society, Lillian felt queasy again. The dream had haunted her into the morning and the only thing she could think to do was to search for more context about the families involved. Perhaps if she found the right piece of history, she could set the ghosts free, move them to peace, somehow. But this building... She tried not to look at those sooty claw-mark handprints on the upper sill.

"A building can't hurt you," she murmured, rallying. "And you are no one but yourself."

The front door opened and a friendly-looking woman, likely in her mid-fifties or so, in a long velvet dress with a floral scarf, waved at her with a welcoming smile. "Hello, are you here for a tour?"

"Hello, well, I'd love to see the place, but specifically, I'm new to town and I'm working with Bethany Glazier in the Persephone Publications archive, and she told me you were hiring in your archives as well?" Lillian stepped up to the front door and offered her resume.

"Oh! Fantastic, I was hoping she'd send me someone!" The woman took the paper, glancing at it. "Hello Lillian Anders!" She offered her hand. They shook. "I'm Carmen Guidano, I'm the Historical Society director here.

Welcome to one of the Denny mansions! This was the home of Eustus and Geraldine Denny, built in 1870. Their extended family would build other mansions further up the hillside in the next decades. Come into my office!"

The building's interior was grand and opulent, with carved woodwork everywhere, bright tiles and gilded surfaces, like it was trying too hard. Lillian's stomach turned again, this time serving up a bitter taste in her mouth. But the bitterness of the house was offset by Carmen's enthusiasm and warmth. If the house made her uneasy, its director did the opposite.

A small room off the main foyer had been converted into an office with a desk and the director bid Lillian sit as she looked over her resume. Lillian noticed a huge painting on the wall showing a grand factory building with DENNY SILVER MFG painted in letters across its brick façade. On Carmen's desk, she noticed a bobble-headed dog, a tall mug holding pens and a pride flag, a painted rock that said *smile* and a few seashells.

"I'm impressed with your background," the director said, referencing Lillian's resume, "and I'm especially excited that you're working on the Glazier archive as well, I think that could really work to our advantage. I don't know if you know much about the history of the families."

"I'm just learning, but there seems to have been some animosity in the past."

"Indeed. But that's behind everyone now, at least I hope so. Now, we can just focus on history and preservation of architecture and records. Can I ask you about something difficult?"

Lillian braced herself. "Sure?"

"The death in the mine… I don't mean to pry, but is Bethany all right? She's *so* smart and sweet, and she's working so hard to try to make a go of that old house. I imagine this makes things all the more difficult. Is there anything I could do to help?"

Breathing a sigh of relief, glad that Carmen felt about Bethany as she did, she shrugged. "It's been hard. A woman I'd just met, there for what was supposed to be a creative retreat, went into an unsafe area she'd been warned not to enter, and she fell. Simple as that." She left out the part about unseen hands and pushing. "But it has meant funding has been pulled from the writer's retreat she'd planned there. I'll give her your regards."

"Please do. What a sad situation. The danger signs are there for a reason, I can't imagine why anyone in their right mind wouldn't listen. As for the archives, it's an absolute mess over there, good luck. Not that it's any better over here!" Carmen laughed. "Between here and there, you're going to be bored to death digitizing things, but that's really what we need the most of, and someone to create a timeline as it's done. And to keep an eye on the climate. These old houses, you know."

"I do. And don't worry, I won't be bored. I love learning things as I read. The past is… well, it's home." Lillian had always felt that way but now she couldn't help but wonder if it was even her choice at all, or if it was all some sort of predestined ploy.

"You'll find a lot of folks here in Glazier's Gap who feel similarly. Everyone says time is funny here. Time and emotions. Everything's just a bit more powerful. Come, let me give you a tour. Let's go top to bottom."

Lillian followed as they climbed to the uppermost hallway leading to the turret room. Of course, they'd have to start there. Maybe this wasn't the room they'd imprisoned Camille in, if there were other family mansions, perhaps it was another turret.

In the unfurnished room, a circular space with wooden floors and leaded glass windows curving out over Main Street below, from this vantage point, the turret looked right across the opposite mountain pass to the Glazier Mansion, the thick curtains of the windows drawn and pinned in such a way that it looked like it was narrowing its eyes at the "rival" mansion.

The door to the widow's walk was closed and barricaded with a wooden beam.

The director began talking about the history of the Denny family; having arrived as manufacturers in the mid-19th century once the mine was into production, positioning themselves as the premier maker of mirrors, silverware, candlesticks, platters, everything people could want out of silver, placing their factory a mile south, just off Main Street in the middle of a rocky clearing where the mountain opened up into a partial plateau.

Her voice faded out as Lillian remembered sobbing in the center of the floor.

In her bleeding hands was a torn ballgown, the sides of her palms worn bloody from pounding them on the wooden door.

Lillian wavered on her feet and Carmen steadied Lillian's shoulder. "I bet you're still getting used to the elevation out here," she said warmly. "Take it easy."

In a gothic arched mirror behind the director, Lillian saw a haggard, bloody Camille in her own reflection.

Camille opened her mouth slowly and screamed "GET OUT."

Carmen followed her eyes to the mirror and held out her hands towards Lillian as she scrambled back out into the hallway, away from the turret room entirely. The director followed Lillian with a rushed, apologetic response.

"Oh! Yes, this building is haunted as well, sorry. Did you see something? The hauntings are right there on our website, so I didn't think to mention them. Truthfully, it's the only thing keeping our doors open, the ghost tours. So, you know, we learn to live with them. Are you ok?"

Lillian nodded, bracing herself against the wall outside. "I'm sorry, I don't mean to seem flighty. Insomnia has been getting to me. And you're right, I think the elevation too." As they descended again, Lillian caught her breath. "Wh… who is that room haunted by?"

"Some say Camille Denny, others say the witch that moved in after her death."

"The witch?"

"That's just what the town called her. She was a cleaning lady who had worked for the Glazier family, always a bit odd. You know towns and rumors about their spinsters. She moved into the turret room a little while after Camille died, hired on to be another cleaner here. But after she moved in, things started going more poorly for the Denny family. Part of their downturn was due to investment speculation, a poor market and a number of unwise decisions, but of course, folks love to blame an old woman with a penchant for herbs and candles. But it was odd they all got sick at the same time. Like the walking dead for a while. Eustus grew *very* ill, and some say he turned to, well… unconventional cures. He died three months to the day after Camille did."

Once back downstairs, Lillian felt immediately better. Carmen led her into a room filled with boxes of newspapers. "This will be your new home for as many hours as you'd like it! We're closing up for the day, but come back tomorrow and you can start right in at any point during our open hours. I'm flexible, so just figure out a schedule between the two archives. I won't be able to pay New York rates, but…"

"That's all right, I don't pay New York rent here either. Thank you. Oh, does that witch have a name?"

"Not that I've been able to find yet. But I've only been here a year myself and only gained access to all the paperwork a few months ago. The Denny family was terrible with keeping records, especially of anyone who was *staff*. Again, I'm not saying she was a witch. I'm not interested in adding to urban legends. But it is something you could look for; anything about her. I'd like to have as much of a full picture of historical class dynamics in the town and how that affects us all today."

Lillian nodded. "I'd like that too. Class dynamics were my focus in the historic narratives I worked with in New York."

"Fantastic. Glad to have you. We'll fill out paperwork next time you're here." Carmen held out her hand again.

Lillian took it and shook firmly. "Glad to be here. Thank you for the warm welcome."

And she *was* glad. If this was where abuses happened, it wasn't the house's fault, or this woman's fault. Lillian wondered if she could be an instrument of helping this house rid itself of its own psychic scars.

Touching the wooden doorframe of the archive room, she patted it, thinking *we're going to be a team, you and I.* She'd said this to the historic house museum in New York and the feeling she had working there after that was a lot more focused and positive. Her last day working there, she'd touched the wall and told it goodbye. She thought she'd heard it murmur, softly, that it would miss her. Maybe that was just her sentimentality speaking. Regardless, treating a building like its own entity was something that had brought her a profound sense of place and peace. It was a measure of taking control over how a place or its history affected her.

She needed to open a local bank account to deposit checks, so she took a walk down sloping, curving Main Street to find the closest option. It occurred to her that as she walked, every road she'd been on in Glazier's

Gap was on a curve, as if nothing here were linear. Time and space, all in relative dimension.

There were other passersby out and about, traffic was light, but people were hiking, jogging or walking, everyone seeming lost in their own little worlds. But looking around at the slopes and trees on either side of her, one could either look at it as something like walls closing in, as she'd considered yesterday at the picnic tables, or possibly look at it differently: cozy and protected. For all the strangeness she'd encountered, there was still something gratifying about being here. She just had to cultivate that latter feeling. One of the things that had drawn her to being goth was the idea of embracing strangeness and macabre fascinations as an empowering, joyful, even *defiant* act.

For all the concerns, drama and terror of the past days, there was also excitement. If she were being honest, what had happened with William's ghost, and the dreams that haunted her, made her heart race like a schoolgirl. Images of their intimacy, whether memory or dream she couldn't tell, replayed in her mind deliciously. If she had nothing else to call her own, there was at least this echo of a love-affair; seductive in its unfinished business. It could make for an achingly pining narrative in a piece of writing. Angst had its appeal.

The large timber building with *Antiques* in bold letters across a clapboard sign still had their *closed* sign out. Lillian looked forward to going in when it was open. The Blue Taper bar, the next building over, had its front doors open and a couple sat laughing over drinks, lounging outside on a sunny deck that faced the forested slope behind the bar, never minding the gnarled tangle of rocks and upended trees up the slope in the distance.

A small credit union in a squat brick building sat a quarter mile down the sloping curve of Main. Setting up an account, Lillian felt for the first time like a "local" and appreciated that the two tellers each had their own very individual, divergent style, as if a bit of quirk was a fundamental part of living here.

Back in the carriage house, having curled up with a cup of tea, she soon fell asleep.

The dreams, or memories, took over again and she did not fight them.

She wanted to know everything she could about the histories of the families, however the information chose to present itself.

William was standing in the doorway in shirtsleeves, staring at her warmly, hungrily. Looking around, she noticed that everything in the carriage house was transformed again to his time. Looking down, she wore a distinct dress, something that looked familiar. But before she could think why that might be, she noticed a bouquet of beautiful orange flowers clustered at her bustline. The jewelweed William's ghost had mentioned up in the clearing, her favorite.

William approached her slowly. It was clear, from his movement and expression, and the way he made her breathless, that they were both absolutely mesmerized by one another. Her heart was so full of love she felt she could burst.

"Am I me, right now, William, or am I her?" Lillian asked softly.

He cupped her face in his hands and did not answer. "I love you and I always will," he murmured.

Sealing his vow, he pressed his lips to hers and began kissing her passionately, expertly, sweeping her against him in a covetous command. She swooned, giving over to this incredible feeling. As his hands caressed her shoulders, sliding down the ribboned edges of her gown, she looked in the mirror over the fireplace.

Dimly, she realized how and where she saw this ballgown before. Bloodied. The reflection in the turret. This gown was the one Camille was imprisoned in...

"William," she drew back. The flowers scattered from her unbound dress. "We have to go. Flee. Now."

"What do you mean? Our escape is planned for two nights hence--"

"No, we have to go *now*--"

A booming knock on the door. A man began screaming. "I know you're in there with that *commoner*, Camille, and I'm going to kill you both!"

"Run!" she whispered to William. He protested, grabbing hold of her protectively. She shoved him off. "Run," she demanded. "If you love me, you will run."

He looked at her, tears in his eyes, and clenched his fists.

"Please," she begged. "I love you. *Go.*"

Cursing, he ran out a narrow back door as she went to open the front door, defiant.

She stared into the furious face of a cruel man. "You do *not* control my heart!" He grabbed her by the hair and began dragging her away as she screamed in pain.

Chapter Eight

LILLIAN AWOKE, BOLT UPRIGHT, DRENCHED in a cold sweat, the blouse and skirt she'd fallen asleep in moist and clinging to her skin. Somehow, she'd made it into bed, tangled under covers. The sliding doors of the bedroom were open. She looked around at the very modernized, cozy carriage house, a place of refuge and love. That Camille had been dragged from this place in particular felt like an egregious violation.

Glancing at a spray of color out of the corner of her eye, turning to the floor in front of the fireplace, her heart began to race again. She got out of bed and darted to the fireplace, kneeling before its great hearth.

There were little orange flowers spread across the rug. Just like those that had fallen out of her dress in the dream. Jewelweed. The past somehow blending with the present. Non-linear time, like the winding streets of the town, everything on a bending curve.

She should be terrified, she knew this. But instead, William's advice came to her like a friend speaking wisdom, remembering the ghost's words when she first saw the Jewelweed up in the heights above the mine: *If you find precious things, hold them close. They'll protect you. Simple things. Favorite things. Anything you love.*

She grabbed the small wildflowers, folded them into a tissue, and set them on the bedroom desk as she changed into a lightweight black sweater with grommets and black laces down the front and a black drawstring skirt in comfortable, flowing layers and uneven, jagged edges. Tying her black lace-up boots, clasping an obsidian obelisk crystal pendant on a silver chain around her neck, she picked up the tissue of wildflowers and tucked them into her bra.

At some point during the morning, Bethany had sent a text noting contractors would be in and out of the main usable rooms of the mansion, doing tests for mold mitigation in the Glazier archives, so Lillian texted back that she'd be at the Historical Society instead.

After a couple of rings of the front bell, Carmen let her in with a smile, this time the woman was in a different bright floral scarf and a flowing dress with large multi-colored roses, a bold and irreverent power-clash in contrast to Lillian's black ensemble.

"Come, let me show you where the most important things are: the snacks and the coffee pot!"

"Yes, please!"

Lillian was led to an anteroom behind the parlor where sets of shelves were stocked with granola, jars of nuts and condiments. A little service station on a sideboard held a microwave, coffee pot, electric kettle and many options of caffeine. Off this anteroom was a staff bathroom.

"The main light switches you'll be responsible for are those in the front hall. We keep the parlor light, entrance foyer light, restroom and dining room light on at all times. Upstairs, only during tours. Oh, I should have mentioned, sorry. We don't open the rooms on the second floor to the public at any time, there's a velvet rope marking it off, but the door marked Do Not Enter, please, do not enter it. It was Eustus Denny's study and it's just… bad news. Very bad energy, so we just don't go in there, no matter how much the paranormal investigators beg us."

"Noted," Lillian said. Even the Denny patriarch's name sent shivers down her spine. Perhaps that was the face of the cruel man in her dream. "I like it down here much better anyway."

"Me too. I love this place, but now and then…" She shuddered, trailing off. Lillian didn't know her well enough to press. "I have to go out for a bit,"

Carmen changed the subject brightly. "Do you mind fielding any visitors? You can tell them when the tour starts, I give the next one at four and they can book paranormal investigations online only, but they're sold out for the next several months."

"Got it."

The door next to the director's office was the library room, filled with bookshelves lined with old books, the center of the floor stacked with boxes, a desk with a computer, scanner and printer against the wall next to the door.

"Start digitizing anywhere, yes?" Lillian asked at the threshold as Carmen slung a purse over her shoulder in the entrance foyer.

"Yes. If you can keep some kind of log, I'd appreciate it. There are blank legal pads and notebooks in the desk drawers."

"Ok!"

Lillian started by beginning to scan and digitize the box of newspapers nearest the door, planning to work her way back. Keeping a log as requested, she skimmed over proud headlines of Denny Manufacturing winning local and international acclaim for their silverware.

After an hour, needing another cup of coffee, she was startled by the reverberate sound of the doorbell.

As she hurried to open the door, ready to give the spiel about the tours, her mouth dropped open at the sight of a familiar, gorgeous man on the steps.

"William?" Lillian squeaked.

Handsome, striking, likely in his early thirties or so, the tall man with a disarming smile looked *exactly* like William. The same wondrously wild, tousled mop of brown hair bounced in the breeze. She would have recognized his distinctive, lovely face, anywhere, but he was dressed in a stylish, modern, button-down shirt in royal blue, with a tailored black vest and black pants. A messenger bag was slung over his shoulder. He was solid. He didn't float. He was real…

"Um… No?" The man replied with a nervous laugh, his dashing smile only widening. "Do I look like a William? I've been told that I do. But you do look… *really* familiar. Hi. I'm Nathaniel Lynd."

"Hi!" Lillian felt her face flush with heat, sure she'd gone scarlet. "Sorry! Yes, you do look… *just* like a William I know."

"You…" He stared at her, warm chestnut eyes sparkling, as if he had suddenly found a treasure he'd thought he'd never see again. He tried to recover himself as Lillian bit her lip, her heart racing for what felt like the thousandth time since she'd come here, only now, it picked up its fastest speed yet. "I… yeah, you just… look familiar. Also. Sorry. I'm not usually this bad with words, I do words for a living. Forgive me." He laughed again, running his hand through that beautiful brown mop of hair and glancing at her sheepishly. He even had William's gestures.

Lillian fought to regain her composure. "I'm Lillian. Are you here for a tour? Ms. Guidano, the director, gives them at four each day. Paranormal overnight investigations are booked up for months."

"I'm actually here to ask about ghost stories. I'm a journalist and writer, currently working on a book about regional ghost stories, traveling around the country, and in doing a little research, I thought there might be really good ghost stories in this town. I'd always meant to come here…" He looked around the outside of the house, as if trying to determine something.

Don't let him go! A panicked whisper sounded in her ear. In the glass of the front door, Lillian could see a wide-eyed Camille reflected back and she swallowed hard.

"Um… Yes. Ghosts! There are… definitely a few. I can tell you what I've heard. I'm not trained to give you a tour, I only *just* started here, but if you want to come in, I can… tell you what I was told?"

"That would be great, thank you! Do you mind if I take notes?"

"Go ahead."

She gestured that they sit in the front entrance hall on a velvet bench by the grand staircase.

"So, you said you just started here, or just moved here?"

"Both," Lillian replied. "I was born in Minnesota, was a New Yorker for over a decade working in museums but this place… presented itself as an opportunity."

"Same here. I'm from Chicago but I've always been drawn to Colorado, and this town literally sort of… called to me on a map when I was scanning an atlas, trying to figure out my next move."

"This town has a certain…" She paused, lost in his face, lost in memories

71

that were welling up like tears of joy and pain… She fought to regain herself. Herself, not Camille, and this man's name was Nathaniel.

"Magnetism," he finished. He was staring at her lips. Were memories rising up for him too? Was this the person the echoes of lost love foretold in hope? How did any of this work?

"Yes," she breathed, looking away, feeling dizzy. "And… um. Some weird things have happened. Even just since I've been here."

He stared at her patiently, waiting for her to go on. She thought about telling him she'd encountered a ghost, a memory, an echo of star-crossed love who looked *just* like him. But just thinking of it, and what this stranger might do with that information, how utterly mad it sounded, was enough to make her shift to a safer, more generic presentation.

"So, this is the Denny mansion, and they gained wealth from manufacturing silver products from the silver mine owned by the Glazier family up the hill. The two families had a… rivalry of sorts and there's a lot of urban legends about curses and family drama. It's thought that a woman who died here, in a fall from the tower, haunts this house…" Lillian trailed off.

She couldn't tell him about William and Camille. If he had something to do with any of this, he'd have to be the one to bring it up, so she wasn't leading him, prompting him. How else could she know if it was genuine? She didn't want to be the same pressing force that William's echo had been in asking her to remember.

"There's also rumors of a witch that lived here too," Lillian continued quickly. "As the Denny family all became very ill after the woman fell from the turret. It's thought maybe it's her haunting the top floor, no one has been able to tell which ghost is active, exactly."

She realized as she'd been talking and he was taking notes, they had unconsciously moved closer together.

"Sorry," Lillian broke away when her knee brushed his. "I'm…"

"I'm *really* captivated," he said, staring at her intently. "I mean, by the story. Why was she imprisoned up there? What did she do?"

"She… loved someone she wasn't supposed to. He wasn't of her class."

"That's tragic," he said sadly, *knowingly*. He shook his head a bit, as if trying to ease out of a dream, and turned to look at his surroundings with renewed interest. "Wow, this place is really beautiful. I've always been obsessed with historic places, like at any moment they might uncover something for me that had been missing. A piece of a puzzle I didn't know I needed solved."

"Me too."

"Because of that, I've always felt a bit restless. Journalism helps, digging into things, but I guess I'm just a questing soul."

"Same."

"Like there was something out there that only I could uncover." He stared at her unflinchingly. "Like there was someone that was going to change everything, a place or a person, a book or a painting, something was going to make it all make sense."

They'd gotten closer again. "Yes," she whispered. The energy between them had grown absolutely electric. She could feel William's kisses on her bare skin, and she closed her eyes.

A key sounding in the front door brought them back to themselves and had them nearly jumping back. Carmen entered and raised an eyebrow, surprised to see Nathaniel. She glanced at Lillian and smirked. "I leave for what, an hour and a half and you've already brought a *boy* over, Miss Anders?"

Lillian stood awkwardly and presented the guest. "This is Nathaniel Lynd. He's writing a book about ghost stories from around the country and Glazier's Gap sort of... called out to him, you could say. Nathaniel, Carmen Guidano, Historical Society director."

Nathaniel stood and extended his hand. "Pleasure to meet you. You've done a great job maintaining all the details. Who doesn't love a tiled mansard roof? And this mahogany balustrade is magnificent. Is that a *Century Guild* fretwork chair in the corner? I've never seen one in person!" He moved to it reverently.

"And he knows his architecture," Carmen said appreciatively.

"I majored in journalism with a minor in design. I'm *particularly* fond of this era."

Carmen followed him to lean in and speak conspiratorially. "Do you want to see the haunted turret room?"

"Obviously!" He exclaimed with a grin. She began leading him upstairs. He turned back, looking down at Lillian. "You coming?"

"No, to be honest, that room gives me the creeps, I've got to get back to work." She hurried away before her blush grew any more telling.

Once inside the safety of the archive room again, she fanned her cheeks. "Don't let him get away..." The whisper at her ear insisted again.

Lillian turned to the glass bookcase, to Camille's wistful expression. "What do you want me to do? If he remembers, he does. If he doesn't, I can't force that!"

Trying to sort papers, she realized she'd just been collating the same loose leaves for a few minutes aimlessly until she heard the sound of footsteps coming back down.

"There really is an unmistakable pall up there," Nathaniel said sadly. He paused outside the open library door. She looked up to see his warm, caring expression, as if he was so glad to see her even though they'd just met, startled anew by the effect he was having on her.

"Thanks for your time, Lillian." He stepped forward and handed her a card. "If you come across other ghost stories, email, call, text, whatever. Please," his voice became suddenly earnest, even desperate. "I'll be here all week, I'd... Like to keep in touch."

"Yes! Let's!"

He stared at her a moment, as if he wanted to say something else. She wanted to launch into so many things, desperate to know what was on his mind; if he was seeing strange things as she had done the moment she arrived in town, what else might be coming to him...

But the creak of the floorboard behind him brought them both back to themselves. Lillian had no idea how to broach the topic of William and Camille without sounding crazy. Chuckling nervously, Nathaniel ducked out, thanking Carmen for her generosity.

Lillian stepped out into the hallway as he went, clenching her fists and having to dig her heels into the carpet to stop herself from running after him.

"He is *cute*," Carmen said after the door closed behind him. Seeing Lillian's startled look, she added. "What, I may be happily married but I still have *eyes*. Besides, Melody won't mind if I eye the *boys*, she knows they're not competition. Still. You, though, what's *your* story? Do you have someone, or should I go get his number for you? Was his number on his card? Let's--"

Lillian blushed and waved her hands. "No! thank you. I…"

"You what? *That's* a blush." Carmen wagged her finger at Lillian. "Blushes are telling, young lady." Lillian laughed and put her hands over her reddened face as Carmen clucked her tongue. "Oh no, you're *smitten*! I know smitten when I see it! I'm going to call him right back and invite him to dinner--"

"No! I'm—I'm confused. I'm… still getting settled. One thing at a time."

Carmen eyed her, unconvinced. "Whatever you say."

But she did want to have dinner with Will—Nathaniel. But, as William's echo himself said, if it's meant to be… She could feel something inside her fighting, struggling, screaming, crying out for a man who had slipped from her grasp once, never again…

Clenching her teeth, she promised herself—and whatever of Camille was powering her and fighting from within—that she'd email Nathaniel tonight to see if he wanted to tour the Glazier mansion in hopes Bethany would be all right with it.

Looking over a few more papers to feel like she'd gotten some work done, a doctor's prescription fell out from within a ledger book. It described treatment for two of the Denny children for an "unknown poison." She placed it to the side. It might be relevant to whatever "witch" accusations were levied there.

Returning to the carriage house for dinner, she received a text from Bethany saying she'd be out until seven but if she wanted to grab a drink after, she'd be game. Lillian was mid-sandwich, mulling over the email she'd write Nathaniel when the doorbell rang. Assuming it was Bethany back early, she swung the door wide and nearly choked seeing that it was Nathaniel standing at the doorstep. William had come for her.

Chapter Nine

"OH!" NATHANIEL SEEMED JUST AS surprised to see Lillian as she was to see him, but also delighted. Lillian's heart soared as he rambled nervously. "Hi! Lillian! I… was just… over at the Glazier Mansion, seeing if anyone was there and no one answered. Sorry, I saw a light on and thought maybe whoever was here would be the person to let me in. Not realizing that it would be… You. I promise I'm not trying to be creepy, but I realize that having found you, alone, in two historic places in the span of a day *is*, like, actually creepy."

His expression was so endearing, so awkward, and all she wanted to do was give him a hug. And more. She couldn't help but grin. His presence made her absolutely giddy. "I mean, it is odd," Lillian agreed. "I guess we're meant to know each other! But, funny, I was just about to email you. The Glazier mansion might also be haunted." She didn't say *by you* but wanted to. "I'd definitely suggest a tour when Bethany is back. She keeps the parlor light on if she's home."

"Great! I'd love to find out everything I can and make decisions about what will go into my chapter."

"How long will you be here? You said what, a week?"

He stared at her again, and God, it was like she'd been waiting to stare into those eyes all her life.

"As long as it takes." His answer to her question didn't sound like it was about time but rather about her.

They stood there for a long, silent moment. She hesitated about inviting him in, he was a stranger, after all, but… this was maybe her one chance to figure out, once and for all, if there was something to this past life thing or if it would just pass as a bunch of coincidences and an overactive imagination. Plus, if he somehow was her true-and-fated-love, if she didn't take a chance to get to know him and ended up letting him casually slip away, she'd forever wonder why she didn't take a leap of faith in this moment.

She was pretty good about reading energies, and Nathaniel Lynd read as very kind. He smiled at her, as if demonstrating the quality. Was there ever anything so beautiful in the world as a deeply kind man?

Lillian gestured inside. "I just put on a pot of coffee if you want a cup. I don't have the key to the mansion, only Bethany does. But she'll be back soon, so if you want to wait here, I could ask her when she's back."

"Yes, thanks! I don't mean to be any trouble."

"You're… not. Come in."

He looked around as he entered, hanging his messenger bag on the coat-tree by the door. Noting that she had her shoes by the door, he took his off and strode into the center of the room, taking in as many details as he could. "Wow. This looks really familiar too. I'm having the most *consistent* déjà vu I've ever had. It happened the moment I drove in and it… hasn't really stopped."

"Yeah. Happened to me too when I got here."

With him standing there, the fireplace behind him, Camille's warmest memories began blending with hers again. She remembered the crash of passionate clutches and hungry kisses the *moment* her and William managed to escape watchful eyes. Blushing furiously, Lillian noticed Nathaniel staring at her with a fond, almost wistful expression.

Mortified to be so visibly affected by his presence here, she turned away. "How do you like your coffee?"

"Just black, thank you. Oh my God!"

Lillian whirled back to him. "What?"

He was staring, wide-eyed at the photo of William and Camille on the fireplace mantel. "This?!"

"Oh. That. I… well." Lillian had forgotten she'd put it up there. Had she put it up there, even? Her mind felt like a fog. "That was in the archives of the Glazier mansion."

"Its… *us*."

"Yeah? Sort of?"

"I mean, not us, I mean, we're here, but I…"

"It's William Hart and Camille Denny. The lovers who were kept apart in the 1880s. She died trying to get to him. He died of a broken heart."

Lillian approached and shoved the coffee at him, trying not to show how much she was actually shaking. As he took the coffee, their hands touched. In an electric moment that blurred her vision, all Lillian could sense was William's hands roving over Camille and how wondrous that felt. Her senses cleared again at the sound of Nathaniel hissing as hot coffee spilled onto his hand.

"Sorry, I--" they both said at once, stopping to stare at each other, wide-eyed.

"I know this will sound weird," Nathaniel began carefully, "and I'm not usually honest with people I've just met about things like this…"

"Nothing will sound weird, trust me--"

"I feel like I'm having… *memories* that aren't *mine*."

"Yes." Lillian breathed an enormous sigh of relief. "Ok. So, I'm not going crazy."

"Well, if you are, then I am. And I appreciate the company." He glanced into the mirror over the mantel and rocked back on his heels. "Um. Lillian… are you… seeing what I'm seeing?"

She turned to see their reflection. They stood in the mirror in period clothes, him dressed in the finest frock coat William owned, still much plainer than the fine ballgown she was reflected in. Lillian was relieved, at least, that she saw herself in a different dress than the one Camille was dragged out in… Lillian couldn't help but admit, looking at them, that they were so beautiful together, their faces so plainly full of hope and—if she was honest—pure love.

"Yes." Lillian swallowed hard. "I see us. In 19th century clothing. It's not the only time that's happened to me here. I've had many visions of... us. Together."

"This is *freaky!*" Nathaniel said excitedly, setting his coffee down on the mantel. Looking at the reflection, then back at Lillian, then back at the reflection, then back at her again. "But it's great. I mean... I feel *amazing*." He turned back and gently cupped her face in his hands. Her eyes fluttered closed, relishing the soft sensuality of his touch; so much better than a memory. "I've never felt better in my whole life. I..." As he trailed off, she opened her eyes again. "I'm sorry. I shouldn't be touching you right now but it's like I can't help it--"

Lillian leaned in and silenced him with a kiss. It was bold of her, not really her style to be so forward, but she was going to burst if she didn't do something. Their kiss became immediately explosive.

He wrapped his arms around her in a ferocious, passionate clutch as they deepened the kiss, ravenous and gasping. A-hundred-and-fifty-years-worth of waiting and aching thundered in, a roiling tide dragging them helplessly under.

Holding her tightly with one arm, hand clamped around her waist, his other hand caressed her reverently. The loose, wide collar of Lillian's sweater slid down over her shoulders as his fingertips traced every inch of her neck, relishing every angle of her collarbones, following the graze of his fingertips with soft kisses. As he bent her back in his hold, her sweater slid down as his lips traveled down her collar and grazed the collected bouquet of flowers in tissue, orange petals blooming up from the edges of her black lace bra.

"What's this?" Nathaniel asked of the flowers, curious, his hold still strong and steady, his fingertips still reverently traveling over her skin.

"Oh... um... those were my—Camille—Camille's favorite wildflower. I... had a dream of the day you—William—William and Camille got separated. She'd had these flowers in her bosom. They fell out when William was kissing her, just like this actually... In the dream. When I woke up, the flowers... these were here. On the floor. They hadn't been there before."

Nathaniel pulled back but didn't let go of her. "That is... actually terrifying. How could something do that; cross time and space like that?

I mean, that's amazing. But also, maybe a warning we should slow down. Sorry. Wasn't trying to entirely undress you."

He gently pulled the edges of her sweater back over her shoulders but couldn't seem to bear to release her. "I mean, we're *strangers*," he continued. "Even though I feel I've known you all my life. I've had these glimpses of things, memories, and there's always a woman there. I never got a very good look at her, but I knew she meant *everything*. Her dress, there in the mirror, that was what I always saw! I always hoped I'd find her in a painting, some archive…" He reached out for her face again, his face lit with abject, boyhood wonder. "But it's you. I've been looking for *you*. I'm sorry—can I… kiss you again?"

Lillian nodded eagerly. He grabbed her and whisked her onto his lap as he sat in one of the large chairs by the fire, running his hands into her hair and pressing her against the wing of the chair as he kissed her thoroughly. She snaked her arms around his neck and ran her hands into his hair in turn, grabbing hold, the feeling so familiar and so delicious, their breaths and soft sighs urging them on to further caresses that began traveling more boldly. His hand hovered at the waistline of her skirt, hesitating and he drew back with a hissing moan, their ragged breaths and mussed hair making them look like they had been delightfully mauled.

"I'm not going any further because I'd like to think *I* am a gentleman, and if there is a 19th century gentleman inhabiting my body, I'd like to do right by him too. *And* also, considering all the strange and potentially haunted aspects of the day, *this* is the part in the horror movie when the young lovers should slow down and protect themselves."

Lillian closed her eyes and clenched her fists to keep from grabbing him again. "You are… wise."

"But all I want to do is continue." He dove to kiss her neck again and she threw her arms back around him in agreement. "I am starved for you…"

Bethany's car pulled into the drive outside. Lillian jumped at the sound, drawing back from him.

"What, I'm sorry, this is so crazy." Nathaniel's expression was rueful as Lillian adjusted her shirt again. "I really don't want to go too far if you don't--"

"No, it's ok, you're…" She shuddered in delight. "*Wonderful*. But the circumstances in which Camille was separated from William, in this building, has me jumpy. I had a memory of being dragged out of here by my hair."

"Oh, God, that's terrible."

"I do think we have to be careful. There's a curse in this town and I don't know what all, or who all, it will affect. If you've anything sacred, precious to you, talismanic, keep it close. Whatever forces were at work against William and Camille, I don't know if they're against us now, but I'm not sure the brutality that tore them apart ever left the town."

Reflexively, he reached out and squeezed her hand. "All right. I am at your command. I don't know what to think other than I want to know what this…" he gestured between them, "is."

"As do I. That car was Bethany coming back. If you want to see the Glazier mansion, I think I can arrange it, just let me talk to her first."

Lillian stood, adjusting herself in the mirror. It was Camille in the reflection putting her coiffure back together, so she approximated the same top knot and smiled, seeing Camille's blissful expression, not sure where her own ended and Camille's began as the bliss was most certainly shared. Nathaniel did the same, trying to smooth his mussed hair—a lost cause— standing behind her, stealing a kiss on the revealed back of her neck as she swept up her undone hair. The small, delicious act made her gasp, which, she saw in the reflection, made him grin triumphantly as if he'd won a prize.

"Talisman…" he said aloud, thinking a moment. Darting to his messenger bag, he returned with something in his palm, showing it to Lillian. An antique cameo, very similar to one Camille was wearing in the photo on the mantel.

"I found this at an antique shop when I first started this ghost book, and I hoped it was a sign. I started the book because I had been increasingly haunted by the images I told you about. I wanted to see if I could find who was haunting me. This reminded me of someone I couldn't remember." He looked between the mirror and back to Lillian. "Now, I think we know. Camille. You. Whatever this is between us. So, this will be my talisman as you suggested. You've your flowers." He placed a gentle finger to the edge of the blossoms tucked back beneath her shirt. "And I've an approximation of your portrait." He tapped the cameo. He tucked it in the pocket of his black vest and patted it against his heart.

"Wonderful." She pressed her hand against his pocket, lingering there to feel the strong thrum of his heartbeat. "Now wait here," Lillian said, going to the door. "I'll only be a moment."

Nathaniel grabbed his coffee again and sat in the chair with a pleasant smile. "I'll be here."

At the door, Lillian had to force herself to physically move, to exit. She didn't want to be apart from him. Her entire body screamed that now that she had him again, she wouldn't ever let him go. But that felt and seemed desperate. She couldn't lead with that dynamic from moment one. What they knew of one another were old memories and none shaped by *this* world. They needed to establish their here and now, not their past way 'round.

Ringing the front bell of the Glazier mansion, Lillian adjusted herself again, still shaking, but more vibrating with energy, joy, excitement and pent-up desire.

When Bethany opened the door, she took one look at Lillian and knew something was up. "Hi…"

"I've had a weird day," Lillian confessed as Bethany gestured her inside and to the parlor, where Lillian sank into a brocade chair. "I'm… affected. Major coincidences have happened and that's… making me a little scatter-brained, I'm sorry."

Bethany sat on a settee across from her. "No, don't apologize, it's what happens here, sometimes. People can either take this town or they can't. Anita and Serenity are up in their rooms, working on their respective projects because they themselves got overwhelmed by the energies of the area. When you saw the ghost in the house, I figured you'd be cool--"

"And I am, I am cool. Just, excited by all of it, really."

"Ok. I'm trying to get used to it too. It's different coming here as an adult. I notice things I didn't notice as a kid. And I'm trying to tell myself I don't need to be scared. Just aware."

"Agreed. Do you mind if I gave a new friend a tour of the mansion?"
Bethany raised an eyebrow. "A new friend?"

"His name is Nathaniel Lynd, he's a journalist writing a book on ghost stories around the country. I met him at the Historical Society today. He's... very nice."

"Tomorrow would be better than tonight. I'm really tired, and I've got to get on a call now with a new financier while it's still early enough in LA."

"Ok." Lillian nodded and headed towards the door. "I'll go tell him."

"Oh, he's here?"

Lillian blushed. "Yes, he came over to see the house without calling, just checking out the premises. When he saw the light was on in the carriage house, he asked me about the mansion."

"I see..." Bethany eyed her, and Lillian realized she had no capacity to hide anything on her face. Her blush was bright, her eyes were wide, the tell-tale signs of smitten had to be all over her, just like Ms. Guidano had immediately noticed.

"And I should warn you," Lillian blurted, "He looks *just* like the ghost we've seen. In your house. Who I believe is William Hart. And... I've seen the ghost in the carriage house, where he used to live. He was there. In my dreams. So..."

"So... this Nathaniel looks just like the *ghost*, but the ghost has now... been in your *dreams*?"

"Yes. And... I... if you look at an old photo... look a lot, exactly like... Camille Denny. There was a picture of William and Camille in the back of *The Curse* that I found in the archive."

"*Weird.*"

"And Nathaniel saw that photo. And then we saw ourselves, looking like the photo, but in the mirror. Reflected. I know. It sounds *insane*. We're stunned and trying to process it."

"Wow, I bet. So, is this why you were asking about past lives?"

"Yes. I think we're only scratching the surface. But hey," Lillian laughed, realizing she sounded a bit unhinged, "who wants a boring life, eh? I always wanted some portal-time-travel-Victorian-ghost-romance to happen to me. Be careful what you wish for!"

Bethany laughed wearily. "I guess so! See you tomorrow evening. Six is good. We'll give Mr. Lynd a tour then we can snag dinner and talk as much ghost stories as any of us can handle." She eyed Lillian again. "Have fun...

Be safe…"

"I will."

Lillian nearly ran back out the door, pausing and carefully opening the door rather than tearing through it to pounce on him, which would have been her preference, honestly.

Opening the door, she quietly closed it behind her. Inside, Nathaniel was in tears, sitting on the sofa, hunched over. He must have lit a fire as it blazed in the hearth, making the tears glimmer on his striking face.

"What happened?" Lillian exclaimed, rushing over.

"I'm sorry," he said, wiping his cheeks. "I just… Being here. Here in the old house. I remember everything. It's *all* come back. How this place was our haven, our respite, our little castle. How nothing else mattered when we were here together. How much we *loved--*" He stopped abruptly, clenching his fists. "I saw you—Camille… dragged away from here, like you said. It tore me in two. Has it… all come back to you?"

She sat down next to him. "Only pieces. I don't know what to let in and what to block out."

"There's *so* much pain, I don't know where to put it." He turned to gently grasp Lillian by the shoulders. "But there's so much *more* joy at seeing you. But I feel like I'm losing my mind. Because I've lived a life as Nathaniel, not as William."

"And I'm Lillian, not Camille. Its dizzying."

"It's like I *don't* know who I am and suddenly *everything* makes sense. At the same time."

"Exactly!" Falling into an embrace, Lillian grabbed hold of him, as if for dear life. "Thank you," she murmured against his ear. "For helping me figure this out."

"I feel like I'd do anything for you."

"I know William told Camille that. I'll do my best to earn it, even if we just… you know—" she pulled back shyly, "—end up being close friends."

He clenched his jaw and leaned against her cheek, murmuring in her ear. "Oh, I hope it doesn't come to that…" Sliding his arm around her waist, a sensation that felt so absolutely natural and right, like he'd done it a thousand times, he seared her jawline with a dragging kiss. She melted against him, with the same sense of familiarity.

She eyed him. Glancing down at his other hand, which was gently cupping her knee, she noticed a simple silver band on his pinky finger. Not that that indicated anything, but it made her think. Shifting to press her forehead against his, she couldn't bear to fully break away but had to ask an important question. "You don't... have a partner, a person, though, right? You're... free to be here, like this?"

"I do not have a partner. I've been single for about a year. No one interested me. Another reason why I went on the road. I had the distinct sense someone was out there, and I was going to find what was, I hoped, waiting for me." He shifted to kiss her forehead, drawing back with a hesitant smile. "How about you? I mean, do I have to fight anyone?" He put up mock fists and shook his head with a snicker, putting his hands together in prayer instead. "Please, I'm a terrible fighter, I don't want the drama, please say you're single."

Lillian laughed. "I ended the soulless, on-again-off-again relationship the day I knew I had to leave New York. But it had been done long before then."

"Good."

They stared at each other, weighing their options, as if debating whether or not to be sensible. Mutually, they leapt on one another instead, falling back onto the sofa in another round of deep kisses and searing caresses. As Nathaniel pinned her down and she shifted beneath him, arching up so that she could press her whole body closer, she was well aware of his desire, and he gritted his teeth with a groan.

"I don't want to stop but..." Nathaniel drew back, his brow furrowed as he looked down at her.

"We should." Lillian agreed. "If we're going to get to know one another, truly, for who we are, not just driven by glimpses of a past..."

"It would be best not to get ahead of ourselves. Intimately." He sat back and helped her up to sit next to him.

"We are wise and I'm proud of us." Lillian chuckled. Her hand reached out for his knee as she leaned closer. "Even though it's very difficult to keep my hands off you."

He stared at her hungrily. "Glad it isn't just me."

"And even though William and Camille would… like us to continue…'" Lillian shivered, overwhelmed by a particularly scorching memory.

Nathaniel turned to the mirror, even though from this angle they couldn't see the reflection. "You've waited a hundred and fifty years, you can wait a bit longer for *us* to catch up!" He admonished playfully. Lillian laughed. He turned to her, gently tucking her shirt back up around her shoulders, fumbling with a fallen lock of hair. "How about we get some dinner? Can I buy you dinner?"

"Yes! I've wanted to go to The Blue Taper. I bet the bartender has some ghost stories."

"Brilliant."

As they walked down the sloping curve of Glazier Drive, Nathaniel took time to just take in the surroundings.

"I remember this. This walk, down this drive. William tried at every moment to catch a glimpse of Camille."

"Do you remember when they met?" Lillian asked. "I feel like they met when he taught her how to ride a horse, but I'd like to remember the first--"

Nathaniel snapped his fingers. "Yes! I can see it. William was with one of the Glazier family horses, trying to get a stone--"

"Out from her hoof," Lillian said, the moment coming back to her in such a rush she wavered on her feet. "And William was so sweet and tender with the mare I—Camille—just watched for a long time until he noticed. When he saw her and smiled, she was done for. When he touched her gently, helping her up to the horse, she was his. She never cared one whit about his class, status, or money, his loving kindness was everything…" Lillian trailed off, tears in her eyes.

As they stood at the end of the drive, Nathaniel pointed to a darkened window on the southernmost part of the Denny mansion. "Before Camille was imprisoned, she'd stand in her window, candles lit, and every night she could manage, she'd tie a love note--"

"Around a rock and throw it into the street for William to find," Lillian continued, remembering how her heart soared seeing his silhouette on bright, moonlit nights at the base of Glazier Drive, how throwing the rock felt like she was casting a wish towards freedom. "He kept them all, treasured every note, but she burned them all in the carriage house fireplace one night--"

"Because she was afraid they'd be found and he'd be punished," Nathaniel finished. "She was always thinking of his safety, more than her own."

They stared at one another at the base of Glazier Drive, the weight of lifetimes between them.

"There's just so much to feel," Lillian whispered, wiping her eyes again.

"There is," Nathaniel said simply. He reached out, grasped her hands and squeezed them tightly. "And we'll have to feel it as it comes. Share memories as we remember them."

"And be sure to make new ones."

"*And* be sure to make new ones!" he echoed triumphantly.

They turned down Main Street and continued strolling.

Lillian found herself at a loss for words, but Nathaniel saved the day, announcing: "All right, Lillian Anders, get ready for some rapid-fire-getting-to-know-you-the-*you*-in-this-twenty-first-century questions! Favorite color— wait I already know this—black. Favorite band--"

"Depeche Mode."

He stared at her.

"What?" She put her fists up playfully. "*Consistently* good music since the 80s and still going strong, fight me. My dear friend Jillian says, "embrace your cliches" and I do, ok? What about you, hot shot?"

"Doctor Teeth and the Electric Mayhem."

Lillian raised an eyebrow. "The Muppet band?!"

"Oh, don't tell me you don't love Muppets, Lillian, that'll be a deal-breaker--"

"I *do* love Muppets--"

"But really David Bowie."

"Ok, you can stay. Favorite movie?"

"Night of the Living Dead; a *vitally* important societal critique. You?"

"The Muppet Christmas Carol," she declared. It was his turn to stare. "Nathaniel. It is *the best* literary adaptation of all time. The Great Gonzo as Charles Dickens and Kermit the Frog as Bob Cratchit is *the greatest* casting call of all time. I *do* love Muppets--"

"I mean, no argument here! Favorite artist?"

"Gustave Doré."

"Of course," Nathaniel chuckled, "Illustrator of *The Raven*. And your favorite poet is Poe--"

"No, Emily Dickinson but my favorite *author* is Poe. He's tied with the Brontë sisters. You? Favorite artist, favorite author?"

"Favorite artist, I can't pick. I love the Arts and Crafts movement and late 19th century design as a whole. Author: Alexandre Dumas. *The Three Musketeers* really spoke to me as a kid. Knowing what I know now about William Hart, I must've felt the commentary on class injustices Dumas wove into the narrative deeply. Any story, really, about people questioning arbitrary class hierarchies really resonated. That makes so much sense, now."

"I think a lot of our favorite things being tied to the nuances of the past—Muppet Christmas Carol *included*—has to have been informed by the 19th century people who chose us as hosts for their memories."

"How'd we do? Are we compatible in *this* life?" His hopeful grin was adorable. They had arrived at The Blue Taper, pausing in the lot out front that didn't have many cars in it.

"So far so good?" she said, equally hopeful.

"You've yet to let me down," he declared, holding the hefty wooden door open for her.

A bell at the door jingled as they entered the long, one-story bar with lots of silver antiques in locked curio cabinets around the perimeter, a central section of tables and booths along the wall. A long, smooth, dark wood bar with worn wooden bar stools was close to the door. A couple of older men sat at the furthest corner, dressed in knit caps and faded flannel, regaling each other with a war story or tall tale.

A tall, muscular, ginger-haired man, likely around their age or a little older, stood behind the bar washing glasses. His arms were tattooed sleeves of various Hammer horror monsters, and his black shirt had a picture of a series of red roses and one white rose spattered with blood. Lillian immediately recognized the image as a Concrete Blonde album artwork. This guy was one of her people.

Looking up, the bartender took in the sight of Lillian and Nathaniel and held his arms out as if welcoming family.

"*Finally,*" he said with a wide smile. "People with some fashion sense around here."

One of the old men gasped, gesturing overdramatically to his faded flannel shirt and knit cap with a tuft of white hair spiking through a hole. "What, you mean you don't like this *haute couture*? John, you break my heart!"

John the bartender put a hand to his heart. "You, Dave, will always be my fashion plate. But let us welcome the newcomers." He turned to Lillian and Nathaniel. "What'll it be?"

They both looked at what was on tap and chorused "Guinness" before turning to one another with another delighted grin.

When John returned with their pints, Lillian volunteered. "I like your Bloodletting shirt."

John clapped triumphantly and started singing the first line of the song. Lillian added the next, Nathaniel the following, until the three chorused joyously.

The old man next to Dave made a face and swiped a hand. "You kids and your rock n' roll."

"That, Merle," John said with an affected, newscaster tone, "was the first four lines of the *classic*, titular song from the 1990 album release that I am presently wearing on my perfectly toned and muscular body. Do have some respect, my septuagenarian friend."

Dave howled a laugh. "Put some actual music on that jukebox and then we'll have some *perfectly toned* respect, kiddo."

"Did they *have* music in the Mesozoic era, Dave?" John taunted before turning back to Lillian and Nathaniel with a grin. "Don't mind the dinosaurs."

Merle folded his arms into a T-Rex impression and waved them with a little Jurassic growl. Lillian laughed. The elder men turned back to one another and dove into another tall, animated tale.

John came over to Lillian and Nathaniel's side of the bar with menus and a bowl of peanuts. "So, what brings you two into town?"

"Work," Lillian said.

"Ghosts," Nathaniel said at the same time.

"Ghosts here too," Lillian added.

"Uncanny things we're trying to figure out," Nathaniel continued. "A *lot* of déjà vu."

"You'll find that happens here, if you're tuned in," John said quietly.

"Tuned in to what?" Lillian matched his quiet tone, eager to know what someone who had been here a while felt was or wasn't normal. He eyed her, as if judging if she could be trusted. "I mean, I believe you, like this place has a sort of... magnifier of a sixth sense, if you've got any capacity for it?"

"That, precisely. It's different for everyone. And some folks go on blissfully unaware."

"Or a whole new life opens up for you," Nathaniel murmured. Absently, his hand reached out and grazed the small of Lillian's back and a thrill raced up her spine.

"Doors where there used to be walls," John stated. Nathaniel nodded.

Lillian glanced at the appetizers on the menu and pointing to a baked potato. That's all her nerves and the butterflies in her stomach could handle. John made a note of their order when Nathaniel decided on a sandwich.

"Nathaniel is working on a book of ghost stories. I figured you'd have to have heard some, if you don't mind sharing?" Lillian asked.

John snickered. "Sure. Every place has ghosts. The old lodge, I mean, I'm sure you can see the damage from the avalanche, it just being left there has been a... spectral gravity well. The ski lifts are weird, sometimes they move even though the mechanism's been down for years. Something in *this* building likes to rearrange my glassware. And of course, the big mansions of the old head honchos of the town. I've not been in any of them, just never got around to it I guess, but I've definitely heard they're haunted. Then there's the mine. *That's* haunted. I'm sure you heard about the fall recently."

"Yeah," Lillian gulped. "I was the one that heard the scream, saw the blood and called it in."

"Oh, damn, I'm so sorry," John murmured. He grabbed another pint glass and began another pour.

"Thanks. It was absolutely awful."

John set another Guinness in front of her. "On the house. God. What a welcome."

"That's what the detective said. But it was stupid, though, they shouldn't have been up there, they did know better."

"Where are you staying, if you don't mind my asking?" John continued.

"Near the Glazier mansion," Lillian replied.

"One of the Denny mansions," Nathaniel answered. "Not the historical society but a smaller residence further up the hill."

John nodded slowly, as if weighing what to say.

"How long have you bartended here?" Lillian asked.

"Since I was young. It's my dad's place. Lived here all my life. I mean, I've traveled. I've seen the world, mind you, but this place, well, let's just say—" he nodded at Lillian, "—from one 'child of the night' to another, calls a person back."

"What about a curse?" Lillian asked, leaning in. "Is there a curse involving the major families?"

John shrugged. "That depends on who you talk to. Everyone has theories but it's not like either the Dennys or the Glaziers ever really got to know the rest of the town. They just lorded over it, one way or another, until the descendants mostly left. Bethany, though, she's great. I'm psyched she's getting the old press going again."

"Yes, I'm working with her!" Lillian said excitedly.

"Give her my regards."

"So, the curse, in your opinion, is more urban legend to explain bad things happening rather than a foregone conclusion?" Nathaniel asked.

"I think it's conditional."

"Conditional?" Lillian furrowed her brow, tending to her drink.

"There are conditions with any haunting or 'curse,' if you can call it that. At least, that's been my experience. You'll be ok in that mansion if you're working with Bethany, because you'd be seen as family, extended Glazier family. Someone else, outside of your circle, won't have the same experience."

"Conditionally haunted…" Lillian echoed the concept, mulling it over.

"Yes. Everything and everyone in this town is. You have to find your way to make your peace with it. Or it won't make peace with you." He glanced out the window, up towards a bright moon. "Everyone's in their own little world." He turned back to them. "Except for me. My job is to know everyone's world but not share it. I am, by decree of this job, neutral. Switzerland. But everyone else may take sides. It may not be their fault. It may be what's haunting them. What part of their past is catching up to them." He looked between Lillian and Nathaniel. "Something brought you two here."

"Yes, it did. And I'm glad," Nathaniel said, staring at Lillian openly. She glanced at him and smiled, her hand questing for his, squeezing it under the bar.

"Just keep an eye out," John cautioned. "I know the Denny family has been doing well renting out their mansions and they're all beautiful buildings, but my advice, regarding a curse, is if you get a bad vibe, bail. Those old houses have minds of their own."

Their food came quickly, and John got drawn into refereeing which man, Dave or Merle, had the more believable Bigfoot encounter out by the scenic overlook up past the old ski slopes.

"Maybe it would be safer if you stayed in the carriage house," Lillian said quietly. "Not that I'm trying to push you to be with me, but--"

Nathaniel leaned in close to her ear. "William's memories have been…. *explicitly detailing* what it means if we stay in the carriage house together. And while I'm *more* than tempted, I want to be sure that's what *we* want. But per John's caution, if I get a bad vibe, I will bail. Promise."

"Thank you, that's all I was saying."

"You too, though," Nathaniel added. "The carriage house might have been our safe-haven, but Camille was still pulled from it."

Lillian shuddered. "We'll have to remain on guard. I wish William's ghost had given me a better idea of how to protect ourselves."

"William's ghost… If the ghost was *separate* from me, what's powering my memories?"

"He appeared to me before you arrived—an echo really, a manifestation of his and Camille's love. Haven't seen him since. Hopefully we can find something in the archives and records that can tell us how we can keep history from repeating itself."

"We're *already* keeping it from doing so. There are no overbearing, violent parents here, keeping us from doing what we want. Maybe us just… finding each other means the curse could finally be broken."

They stared at one another for a long time. Lillian felt Camille's heart overflowing and she didn't know how to translate that here, in a modern bar, with a man she just met.

"There's just so much to feel," Nathaniel echoed her words from earlier. She nodded.

They thanked John as they rose from their seats. Nathaniel treated, insisting as he'd invited, and tipped John well. Both he and Lillian waved to Dave and Merle as they headed for the door.

"Don't get eaten by werewolves, kids," Merle cautioned, pointing a bony finger at them.

"Really? Is that a thing?" Lillian asked John, who shook his head with a chuckle. "I mean, I dunno around here, I'll proceed with caution regardless…"

They exited with a laugh as Merle chastised John for being lackadaisical about a sincere and rising threat.

"The moon *is* full," Nathaniel noted as they stepped out into the night, throwing back his head in a small howl. Lillian laughed but couldn't help but glance around at the dark forest on either side of them, impenetrable even by the bright moon above. It was a place where any legend could flourish.

Wan pools of light below the few streetlamps lining Main led their way back. Nathaniel held his arm out. Lillian took it. *That* felt familiar. She felt them both shudder as if four bodies were registering the connection.

"It's as if I'd done that countless times before," Lillian noted. Nathaniel nodded with that same winning smile that had stopped her heart when she'd first opened the door to him at the historical society.

"I'll walk you back to the carriage house then I'll circle back to the Denny villa."

"That's nice of you, you don't have to come all the way up--"

"Werewolves, remember?" Nathaniel said with a smirk.

They walked in quiet for a few moments, looking around a town that was at once familiar and foreign, quiet in the dark with only the occasional sounds of animals, insects and cars on the county road beyond.

"Tomorrow after six is good for Bethany. She said we can all do dinner," Lillian said as the Glazier mansion loomed before them.

"Great. I'll be at the Historical Society archives, searching for a few specific things, before I come over to the mansion."

Crossing towards the carriage house they lingered at her doorstep. Lillian didn't know what to do with her hands. She wanted to grab him. Instead, she just clutched the sides of her skirt. "I'd invite you in again for a cup of tea or something but…"

"But I would have a very hard time *not* trying to recreate *all* the things I *very* vividly recall William and Camille doing--"

"Yes," Lillian gasped. "That's… been distracting. All-consuming, really." She fanned her blushing face.

Nathaniel leaned in and spoke through clenched teeth. "It's pretty hot, though, you've got to admit."

Lillian turned to his ear with a murmur. "Oh, I do."

"Something to aspire to, perhaps," he said, drawing back with a wink. "But seriously though. Can I ask you something before I go?"

"Sure."

Nathaniel took a deep breath and launched into an absolute torrent. "I mean, I know this is jumping the gun but we already almost tore each other's clothes off and we both remember *every* intimacy, and I'm getting this distinct, okay, desperate feeling from what I assume is the urgings of William, or maybe, you know, maybe it's just me, terrified to lose or mess up a really wonderful thing so I think what I'm hoping for is that you'll say yes in, you know, wanting to be… my girlfriend?"

God, he was adorable. "Are you asking to court me, Mister Lynd?" Lillian exclaimed, a hand to her breast. She leaned in with a seductive smirk. "Exclusively?"

"Yes! Courting! Exclusive courtship." He laughed nervously. "That's the stuff of those old days we're so fond of, isn't it? Jolly good and all. Would you… Can I *court* you, Miss Anders?" He dropped the affect. "No, really though, I need some assurances here you'd like to see me again--"

Lillian grabbed his shirt, pulled him to her and kissed him hard. Wrapping her arms around him, she drew back from the kiss, but pressed her body fully against his.

"That, that's a great answer, Miss Anders."

She grinned. "It was a great question. Consider me officially courted."

"This is *crazy*," he murmured, eyes wide. "But I'm so…"

"Happy!" Lillian said, tears welling up in her eyes as she realized that was the only word for how she felt.

"Yes! Happy! Oh. But does that…ruin your Goth cred though?"

Lillian laughed. "I think 'being an earthly vessel for a consumptive, hundred-and-fifty-year-old-ghost who was torn from her lover and died of a tragic fall trying to get to him' wins back the points."

"Yeah, probably."

She let her arms drop from around him but took his hands in hers instead. "Thank you for being great about… this insanity."

"You too. And if this is wrong, I don't want to be right!" He leaned in to steal one last deep kiss before drawing back and walking away.

Turning back to her, he bowed and then strutted off. She laughed. He kept turning back to her, finally calling just before he was out of sight. "Your *beau* will come calling, Miss Anders, at half past five in the morrow!"

"I shall count the minutes until we are reunited, Mister Lynd," she called back, blowing a kiss. He reached as if fumbling to catch it, grabbing it zealously, pressing it to his lips, and waving. He strode out of view with a jaunty, silly walk. She missed him already.

She closed the door behind her and slid down the back of it, laughing through tears like a maniac.

It took her quite some time to get to sleep. Her thoughts alternated between Camille's thoughts of William, sharing scorching details of their intimacies, and Lillian imagining those same delights with Nathaniel.

Would she see William's ghost again? Or were the echoes, now that they were, essentially, reunited, now left to fade?

There were so many things left to answer, so many things left to wonder about, the sheer metaphysics of it all, but those details were beyond her. All she could do was sigh and pine and toss under her covers, restless and on fire from head to toe. A delicious situation for someone who dearly loved all those aching Victorian novels. Now, to make sure they survived the rigors of one.

Chapter Ten

LILLIAN WAS STARTLED AWAKE BY a loud knock on the carriage house door. She threw on her black velvet robe and stumbled to answer.

Lillian opened the door to see Bethany smiling knowingly at the threshold with a paper-bag breakfast in hand. "Hey there, sleepy head, late night?"

"Hi! I just had a hard time getting to sleep. I didn't miss a meeting or something, did I?"

"No, I just wanted to check in. Past-life-lovers-reunited doing a number on you?"

Lillian chuckled groggily. "Yes. Exactly that." She gestured Bethany in. Thankfully, in her haze, she'd programmed the coffee pot. She poured Bethany a cup as she sat at the dining table.

"Well, I'm looking forward to meeting him, then!" Bethany exclaimed. "Hope he's a keeper. Being saddled with a dud coming back to haunt you would be the worst."

"So far so good," Lillian said, perhaps a bit too suggestively.

"Wait did you…"

"No. Heh. I mean, we almost—it was hard. All our memories, of *them*, you know, doing… *everything*, came back to us, along with everything they felt, so… It was, really intense, and hard, to try to figure out boundaries."

"I bet!"

"We're trying to be sensible. Pace ourselves. But I'll be honest, we did make out. A lot. It was *great*! He's great!" Lillian put her hands over her bright red cheeks. "I feel like a silly schoolgirl, I'm sorry."

Bethany grinned. "No! I love it. Good for you. At least something good has come out of this retreat."

"In all seriousness, Bethany, I like it here and am grateful. Regardless of what happens with Nathaniel. You've helped change my life for the better."

"Aw!" Bethany reached over and squeezed Lillian's hand.

"Now." Lillian placed her palms on the table, trying to ground herself and talk business. "Your archive. As I'm digitizing and sorting, we can also think about arrangement. What you'd like to see done with it. There are several ways you can go in terms of what to store and what you'd like to display."

"Can we talk about it in the room? The contractor set up an air purifier in there just to take some of the dust out."

"Absolutely. Give me one second."

Lillian ducked into her room to throw on a simple black shirt and flowing black cotton slacks. Grabbing her coffee mug, she followed Bethany back to the Glazier mansion.

They crossed through the dim, strange rooms and back to the archive, where they started out by discussing setting up a display of every book Persephone Publications had released, creating a timeline showcase out of one of the glass cabinets.

As they spoke, Bethany's phone dinged.

"Wow. Sally's been discharged from the hospital, and it would appear she's already making videos again."

"Geez…" Lillian made a face. "That's…."

"Everybody's got their own way of coping, I guess, I'm just going to let her do her thing and pray she doesn't blame me for their own stupidity. You going to sort through things in here today or over at the Historical Society?"

As much as she wanted to be where Nathaniel was, she needed to let them each take a breath, separately. "I'd actually like to see if I can find

Glazier staff paperwork. I'd like to see if I can find out anything about William or his family. The ghost talked about the curse, wanting to stop it, so maybe, if somehow our spirits are wrapped up in it, if the curse was set by someone who knew and loved him, maybe we can figure out how to end it."

"Sounds like a plan. Mind if I join you to work in here too?"

"I'd love it!"

Bethany sorted through Persephone Publications records, creating a box of what to recycle and what to keep as reference material. They ordered in lunch from a burrito shop far up the road and talked about what they were looking through as they went.

"Each of the books the press published has an associated box of reference material," Bethany said. "Not every writer stayed here in Glazier's Gap to write the books, but it seems a lot of them did. And I think a lot of the plots and the details were coming from real events, or at least, real urban legends."

"That will be very interesting to sift through," Lillian stated. She referenced the pile of papers, ledgers and daybooks she'd been examining. "I think I'm at least getting a historic handle on the staff side of things here. It really seems like staff was treated like family."

"I'm glad to hear it. There wasn't money for staff any more by the time I was born, this place really was just a glorified office for the publishing house, but at least we don't have any tormented cooks who were treated terribly haunting the house. A hot stable-boy who loved the rich girl across the street is definitely a better ghost than a vengeful scullery maid."

Lillian laughed. "That's the truth! I got a sense from the Historical Society it was a bit opposite over there in the Denny family. Am I right in that the Glaziers came from older money and the Dennys were more, what, nouveau riche?"

"Yes, the name itself originates from the trade, mirror making, which I guess my dad's ancestors did dating back in England to the 17th century. But they worked their way up, somebody became a lord somewhere at some point, and they came here to open the mine when the silver was discovered. The Denny family came later, to make something with it. My grandfather, I remember him saying that the Denny clan always felt they had something to prove. It wouldn't surprise me, then, if they had a harsher class distinction and would demand their children try to follow it."

A white-hot rage burbled up inside Lillian. How dare that family not think William Hart was good enough for their daughter. He had the kindest, most noble, gentle, *kingly* heart a man could have. A bitterness came over Lillian like a dark cloud as Camille recalled the boorish, boring English baronet without any money her parents had demanded she marry for a title.

"You ok over there? You seemed to… go somewhere."

"Oh. Sorry. Memories. Camille has a lot of thoughts on the subject of worthiness, class, and who she did and did *not* want to marry."

"That's got to be wild, when someone else takes over…"

"It's interesting, that's for sure. I'm trying to think about it like I would if I was still in theatre, like I was when I was a kid. Camille is… a character I can channel very well. I don't want to lose that boundary."

"I guess that's a good way to think of it."

Lillian was thankful this was all happening when she was an adult. If she'd been faced with this when she was still trying to figure out who she was and what she wanted—out of life and out of a partner—it would be a lot harder. Even though Lillian had always felt a bit out-of-place while searching for things that felt like "home," she knew what felt good and true when confronted with it. In the end, her instincts were solid, and she felt she could grow and blossom here, defiant against any odds. Nathaniel's kindness, respect and slightly whimsical nature was exactly right; a piece of a puzzle that fit neatly by her side. As long as they remained open and honest, this crazy situation just might work. He didn't seem to shy away from emotion and that was incredibly attractive.

Lillian turned back to the papers, losing herself to the records again. There was such a profound peace in getting lost in minutiae; sorting, searching and getting a timeline.

When the clock in the archives struck five, Lillian jumped up. "I'm going to fix myself up a bit."

"Because your century-old-lover is coming to *call*…" Bethany taunted.

"He looks *really* good for a hundred and fifty years old, I'll have you know." Lillian grinned. Bethany laughed.

She skipped back to the carriage house and changed from the basics she'd worn in the dusty archive room to a voluptuous black dress with gauzy sleeves and a fitted bodice and a sheer overlay billowing out around a sleek, sheath skirt. She placed the obsidian back around her neck. Obsidian was a stone that was good not only for communicating with past lives but in blocking negative energies. And it was black. Goth trifecta. "Stereotype Technology," to quote Jillian again, a wise woman reigning as goth auntie to the world, having written a bible about the care and feeding of the goths in one's life.

Pinning up her hair and adorning the coiffure with satin black rose clips with little fangs in their blossoms, she grabbed the small jewelweed bouquet she'd pressed into the tissue and put it back in her bra again. The flowers were fragrant and comforting. Another silver chain, one that was more of a choker, glimmered from her open jewelry box. She put it around her neck to give the jewelry a more layered look. Increasing the Technology.

Glancing at the clock nervously, she noticed it was after five thirty.

"Late," she pouted in a voice that might have been Camille's, she couldn't be sure.

Stepping outside, she looked around for Nathaniel in case he'd tried the door and was wandering around the grounds, waiting.

Her phone dinged. Bethany texted her a link to one of Sally's videos with Bethany's own comment: "Can you believe this shit?"

In a video that evidently posted earlier in the day, there was Sally, going into a hallway Lillian recognized as the Historical Society. Sally specifically entered the room that was forbidden, the video pausing on the Do Not Enter sign, turning her phone back around to her face, which still sported a bandage and stitches over her cheek.

"As if I *wouldn't*," she scoffed at the sign, turned her phone back around and started poking around the interior of the study. It was a room full of books, papers and framed diagrams of products. There was a large, ornate silver box on the desk, and a hefty, odd book beside it.

"What's this?" she asked. She fumbled with the latch of the silver box and when she opened the hefty lid, an ink-black shadow swooped up and out. It was terrifying. Sally cried out, running back out the way she'd come. "I don't know *what* that was but I'm not staying around to find out!" The video cut to her down the block, sitting catching her breath on one of the tables by the ice cream stand. "There was something bad in that house and I can't wait to get out of this town. Thanks for your well wishes, everyone. I know your love and engagement with us saw me through. I know Cindy would want me to keep going, so I couldn't let her and all of you down by not continuing..." Sally started to cry, at least, it seemed like it, Lillian couldn't be sure what was genuine. "So, I *will* continue. But not in this place. See you back in Cali." The video clicked off.

Lillian shouted at the screen. "You just... opened a *weird* box in a room you weren't supposed to go in, and just... left it?!" She bit her tongue to keep a string of curses at bay.

God. Was Nathaniel still over there?

A squawking in the sky above alerted her to an enormous murmuration of blackbirds moving towards the Denny house. She remembered what the echo of William said to her; that such a gathering was an ill omen.

"Nathaniel..." she murmured and started running towards the house. Running into the street, she narrowly avoided getting hit by a pickup truck.

"Watch where you're running, freak!" the driver cried. Lillian just kept running.

As she approached the old Denny house, only one light was on.

The tower room light.

Her heart pounded. She felt like she was going to throw up. She ran up the front stoop steps and rang the bell. No answer.

"Carmen?" She called against the door. "It's me, Lillian, can I come in?"

No answer.

She called louder. "Nathaniel, are you in there?"

Trying the knob, Lillian was unnerved to find it open.

Looking around, no one was downstairs. But Nathaniel's messenger bag was in the library room. She glanced down at his open notebook, where two sentences scrawled hastily grabbed her attention:

Eustus Denny urban legend? Silver helpful against his angry spirit?

"Nathaniel?" she called, panicked. "Carmen?"

Silence.

Everything inside her screamed to turn around, to try to save herself. She knew that she could not bear that room again, terrified that she wouldn't make it out of there alive. But she *had* to see why that light was on and no one was answering.

As she passed a display case near the base of the stairs, one part of the glass cabinet was open. She recalled when Carmen was first giving her a tour that there had been historic medical implements and bottles of medicines inside, as one of the Denny relatives had been a druggist, but the display case looked like something had been rearranged or removed.

She took a deep breath and spoke inwardly. "Camille… help me. Let's find William. I need you to be strong. We need to be strong, for him. For our love…"

The concept of calling a man she'd just met her love seemed wondrous and ridiculous all at once. But it was true. She ran upstairs as fast as her violently shaking body would let her.

Outside the tower room in the hallway, Carmen lay crumpled on the floor.

"Oh my God." Lillian rushed over to see a silver candelabra lying on the floor beside her, unlit candles thrown out from their holders, a coagulating gash on her forehead and a trickle of blood down the side of her face. Fumbling her fingers on the side of Carmen's neck, she found a pulse. "Thank God."

Full of dread, she turned around. Nathaniel lay on the floor of the tower.

"No, no, no, no…" She ran in and knelt over him. She reached for his pulse. It was there, but it felt faint. She fumbled for her phone before realizing it wasn't with her. Either she left it downstairs, or it got tossed out of her hand when she nearly got ran over. "Damn it."

Fighting back tears, she ran down to the office landline and called for help.

Once she slammed the phone back down after she'd been promised that an ambulance was on its way, she forced her weak knees to race upstairs again.

Turning the corner towards the tower room, there was unexpected company at the threshold.

A ghost floated between her and Nathaniel. A vaporous, sad form trailing into nothingness. Her features were mostly visible, an older woman in a black dress with a white apron.

"Who are you?" Lillian barked. Refusing to let anything keep her from Nathaniel's side, she ran through the ghost to get to him, shuddering as she went through the cold mass.

The spirit whirled on Lillian as she bent over Nathaniel, murmuring his name. Grasping his cold hands, she brought them to her lips. "Nathaniel, stay with me. Please."

"I'm Matilda Hart," the ghost answered. "I used to live here."

Lillian glared up at her. "Hart? A relative of William's?"

The apparition clutched her heart. "His devoted aunt!"

"You're the witch." Lillian tried to warm Nathaniel's hands by rubbing hers against his gently, sliding her hand under his head, trying to rouse him.

The spectral woman pursed her lips. "Everyone said *Witch*, but no, I just believe in simple herbs as cures." She smiled an eerie smile. "And sometimes, poisons are the cure. I made them all sick. To make them think twice about their attitudes."

"So, you created the curse?"

"No, the *actions* of the Denny family proved their own curse. But, just like the ghost of William and Camille's love was made manifest in an echo, so is the ghost of those actions. Their cruelty became its own ghost and when Eustus died, that cruelty merged with him. Becoming something more terrible than a ghost. A true monster. Claws and all. And that beast is hungry. So, you'd best be ready to fight it. Because it's come for him." Matilda gestured to Nathaniel. "It came for me, recognizing my vengeance for what it was. It'll come for you."

"Can you help us?" Lillian begged. "Can we free you too? Let's stop this cycle."

Matilda shrugged. "I'll try. But first you have to wake this poor boy up."

"How? What happened to him?"

The ghost pointed outside, to Carmen.

Lillian shook her head. "No, she wouldn't. She wouldn't hurt anyone."

Hart's smile was terrifying again. "She wasn't *herself*, let's just say. She had a little help from the spirit of Eustus Denny himself. Some little tart let him out of his prison!"

Damn it, Sally, you bitch.

Lillian wondered what she could do to wake Nathaniel. Instinct took over and she reached against her heart and pulled out the blossoms.

"Oh!" Matilda exclaimed, the ghost clapping vaporous hands. "Jewelweed. Dear girl! Camille really has come through to you, hasn't she? Praise be..."

"Nathaniel, please, wake up," Lillian hoisted him closer in her arms, drawing the flower under his nose. "Please. It's me. It's Lillian." Whispering in his hear, she began crying softly. "William, it's Camille... We're going to make it this time. We have to. We *have* to."

He moaned, shuddering. "Yes, please wake," Lillian pleaded. "I need you to stay with me. Camille loves you, William. I'd like to know what that's like. I'd like the chance to love you, Nathaniel, but only if you wake up..." He coughed but nuzzled against her. It would be darling if he wasn't in such danger. Lillian bent down to kiss his temple and he loosed a soft murmur of contentment. "Please wake up, Nathaniel, we *have* to get this right, you and I..."

Suddenly a crawling figure clamped a hand on Lillian's leg, digging in with fingernails.

"You'll *never* leave, you'll *never* win," growled a terrible voice coming out of Carmen's mouth. Her eyes had gone black, soulless and terrible. She was possessed.

She grasped Lillian with hooked fingers, drawing blood. Lillian kicked her off, scrambling back frantically, sliding Nathaniel back with her as best she could, trying to block him with her own body.

Face contorting, Carmen seemed to wrestle within herself. Matilda threw herself at Carmen and she was knocked back away from Lillian.

"This may be your old house, you wretched beast, but these hearts are *not* yours to dominate. Never were, never will be!" Matilda grabbed hold of something, a dark, skeletal frame, trying to pry it away from Carmen, throttling it. "I'll drag you *straight* to hell with me..."

"Emergency services!" Called a voice from below and footsteps charged up the stairs.

Matilda turned, her ghostly form wavering, and she managed enough poltergeist energy to lob the silver candelabra at the silhouette and the dark form vanished, hissing as it went out the hallway window.

Carmen slumped again, unconscious. Nathaniel coughed. As the EMTs rushed in, they gestured Lillian back. "Are you who called?"

"Yes. I think he may have hit his head. And he may be drugged? He's really unresponsive and sluggish."

"Are you hurt?"

"No," she said, shifting her skirt to hide the cut on her leg from Carmen's grasp when she truly hadn't been herself.

The EMTs took his vitals. "Yeah, some kind of sedative or something, we'll have to pump his stomach to be sure. Did you see him take anything?"

"No, I just saw his cup of coffee downstairs, I knew he was working here. We were... supposed to go on a date, he was late... I came to check on him, found him like this."

"And her?" Another EMT was checking on Ms. Guidano.

"She fell? I don't know. She's harmless, she's really nice. No one was trying to hurt anyone here."

The EMTs just looked at her.

Once Nathaniel was taken out on a stretcher, Lillian could hear Carmen in the foyer with the other responder, rousing slightly, crying. As Nathaniel was loaded into the ambulance, Lillian rushed up to the vehicle.

"Can I ride with him, please? He's my... boyfriend." Saying it felt like a thrill and a stab of fear all at once. If she lost him now that she'd found him, she felt sure she'd never recover. Camille certainly wouldn't.

As they rode together, Nathaniel went in and out of lucidity. She held his hand and rubbed it gently, kissing it and murmuring that he was going to be all right if he kept fighting.

Every time he managed to open his eyes and focus on her, his shifting discomfort eased, and his breathing settled, his heart rate leveling out to a normal beep.

"You're good for him," the EMT said quietly, encouraging.

Lillian offered a faint smile. "It's... nice to be good for somebody."

"Amen to that."

The entire experience with Nathaniel and William, her entire experience in Glazier's Gap even, despite the terrors, had given her life a vibrance and meaning that she'd been lacking. Whether she was, actually, channeling Camille or merely the idea of her had awoken something inexplicable, something that could be witnessed in mirrors and memories, destiny had finally found her. She would work hard to make sure she lived into it as best she could.

Nathaniel roused in the ambulance, and she leaned over him, brushing her hand over his wild hair fondly. "Hi," she said gently. "Hang in there."

"Hi," he said with a wan smile. Tears limned his eyes. "I'm so glad you're with me. I'm sorry. I don't know what happened."

"The past isn't going to repeat itself, Nathaniel. Not this time. We're not going to let it."

He closed his eyes, tears falling onto his cheek. Lillian wiped them gently. He turned into her hand. "Love you…" His murmur drifted off into a listless unconsciousness.

Lillian bit her lip and felt her heart could crack right open. It was likely just William talking. But she wouldn't mind if Nathaniel said it too. Love at first sight had maybe never been quite so complicated but it was something Lillian wanted to treasure. One of the things that had drawn her to goth as an aesthetic and subculture wasn't just that she'd been a bit of a traditional melancholiac but the concept of profound emotion, especially concerning love and loss, was welcome. Celebrated. This wellspring had precedent.

At the hospital, Lillian followed along as much as she was able, eventually sitting outside in a chair nervously. She wished she had her phone to call Bethany, text Keri, Jillian, anyone, but her only company was her thoughts.

A mere couple of weeks ago her life had been entirely different. Everything had been upended since then and nothing was familiar. And yet, this man was. Familiar. Family. Inexplicably. His presence was a home she'd been trying to find, that visage seen out of the corner of an eye, waiting for her to turn and acknowledge his importance.

A woman in a lab coat came out, interrupting her deep reverie. "Hello,

I'm Dr. Singh, are you Nathaniel's girlfriend Lillian?" The young doctor's warm smile was a balm and reassurance. "He was asking for you. You can come and see him. He's had his stomach pumped. It was a barbiturate that incapacitated him and he's on an IV. After a bit more monitoring we can discharge him."

"Thank you so much," Lillian replied, fighting back tears.

She ran in. His brown hair was still wild, and he looked pale, but his eyes were bright and the moment he saw her, he opened his arms. She ran to embrace him, careful not to unhook the IV on his arm. "Thank God you're ok," she murmured and kissed his forehead, his temple and grabbed his hands. "Sorry if I'm overdoing it here, I'm just--"

"No, I'm grateful for your care," he replied, launching into another awkward, rambling torrent that made Lillian teary. "I was pretty scared there, I have to admit. I'd just found the love of my life, I mean, I think so, let's say so just for the sake of a great story, and here some sort of damn demon or something, I don't even know, comes at me from that nice lady. I didn't realize she wasn't herself until she asked me upstairs to look at something and when we were up there, she swung a punch at me and missed, but I was dizzy. That's when I realized something must have been slipped into my coffee, because I didn't have any reaction time."

"That's terrible." Lillian wiped her eyes with one hand, keeping hold of his in her other. "What else happened?"

"A voice that *wasn't* Carmen's laughed at me. The voice growled, 'you'll never have Camille, not then, not now, not in any life!' Then I was hit with a candelabra but as I went down, I did see Carmen fight back before she could deal me a worse blow. She hit herself on the head with it instead. That was brave."

Nathaniel stopped talking when a detective came in and eyed Lillian. It was the same detective she'd met before, up by the mine. The detective recognized her immediately. "Weren't you the one who called in the woman who fell?"

"Yes," Lillian replied wearily.

"Well, don't you have the worst luck!"

"Seems so," Lillian countered carefully.

The detective turned to Nathaniel. "So. What happened?"

"Carmen was trying to help me when she... fell."

The detective didn't look convinced. "And the heavy-duty barbiturate?"

"Something was in my coffee. I don't know how that happened. A mix up of coffee creamer? Carmen was trying to help. Something weird happened, definitely, but it wasn't her fault, and I didn't overdose. I promise, I've got a lot to live for." Nathaniel squeezed Lillian's hand, staring at her.

The detective turned to Lillian. "And how did you know he'd be there at the Historical Society?"

"It's where he said he'd be before our meeting, so I just went to see what was holding him up. I work there too. I found him upstairs and called 911."

"I'm going to question Ms. Guidano, who was also brought in. This town is going to be the end of me," he muttered, exiting.

"I have a confession to make, Lillian," Nathaniel said as soon as they were alone again.

Lillian narrowed her eyes at him.

"I opened a book I shouldn't have, in a room Carmen said not to go into."

Lillian punched him on the arm. "Doubly stupid."

"I know, I know. But I was looking for something that was listed in the catalogue of books the Denny family owned: their family history. It wasn't in the archive room, so I went into Eustus Denny's old study. What I found up there on his desk was a grimoire, of sorts. The book had damage from the house fire in the seventies. His 'book of shadows' made it out intact, however. I got a really bad feeling after I opened it. There was an open silver box on the desk. I put the book inside, having read earlier in the archive about Eustus' intense silver allergy."

At this, Lillian ran her hand over her neck. It was providential she'd doubled her necklaces. She unclasped the obsidian pendant on the sterling chain and clasped it around Nathaniel's neck. "Just in case. With the allergy, maybe this can be an element of protection."

"Thank you."

"Anyway, continue."

"I went back to the archive room. Carmen, at least I assume it was her, had set coffee beside my chair. I just drank it without thinking. It didn't set in until she'd asked me upstairs and then, the confrontation, I was in and out of consciousness, now we're here."

Lillian put a hand over her forehead. "Yeah. The open silver box. That went out on a livestream earlier in the day. A very stupid, selfish woman who should *know* better. Because it was *her* colleague that died just days ago in the mine. Did you see her, Sally? Anyone making a video upstairs on the second floor?"

"No, I heard Carmen giving someone else a tour and then they separated. I had the door closed, working. I did hear Carmen mutter about people not reading the signs, but I didn't think anything of it. When I went into the room myself, the grimoire was on the desk. It had a lot of dust on it, so it hadn't been opened recently. But the box was."

"You didn't see a black shadow with claws anywhere?"

"Something dark and shadowy passed over Carmen's face as she was fighting something, but I was nearly out cold at that point."

"So, whatever that thing I saw was, whatever vanished when the EMTs showed up, is still out there."

"Hopefully we can put it back in whatever it came out of?" Nathaniel tried to sit up higher with Lillian helping him. "*The Curse* specifically says if you directly go against something the Glazier family had decreed, you open yourself up to danger. The Dennys had their own version of a curse, so I'm not sure which one applies to our situation. I honestly thought all that just sounded like an urban legend the founders created to keep townspeople beholden to their interests."

"That may be, but William and Camille know better."

"How did you know to use jewelweed to help rouse me?"

Lillian shrugged. "Scent is the most potent memory. Since William's ghost, before I met you, made such a note of it, and when it literally appeared out of nowhere in my house... it seemed like it might carry something a bit more powerful."

They stopped again when the doctor returned. "You look ok, and the sedative is out of your system, so you're free to go. As for the hit on your head, you avoided a concussion somehow. I'm not sure what happened, but be careful with yourself in old houses around here. They're out to get you."

Nathaniel saluted the doctor. "Yes, ma'am, they seem to be. I'll keep a better eye out. Thanks for helping me."

The doctor turned to Lillian. "Watch him."

"Oh, I will."

Alone again, she helped Nathaniel to his feet, and they embraced. "Thank you, Lillian. So much. If you hadn't come for me, I might not have made it."

"Of course. We're… in this together."

"Whether we like it or not."

"I don't like the threats, but I like you."

Nathaniel slid his arm around her waist, thrilling her. "I think you're worth the danger. I think you always have been."

"I don't think you should stay the night in a Denny property."

"I agree."

"Come home with me."

"Yes, please." He grabbed a mint at the nurse's station on the way out to steal a kiss in the hallway. "Should we check on Carmen?"

"She'll be ok. Let's let her be. You told the detective enough to keep her in the clear, and hopefully she won't remember anything. We've got to be careful, because if any of us starts talking 'demons' and 'ghosts,' either the doctors or detectives will send us to a psych ward."

"True. Though if there was one town I've ever been in that needs to reconcile the paranormal, it's here."

"It will have to start with us, then."

Hailing a cab back, they got in and snuggled close.

"I hope you have health insurance," Lillian said, suddenly worried about the logistics of the recent events. "And that it actually pays for something. If I'd have had a car, I'd have driven you, rather than the ambulance--"

"I'm good. I'll be fine. My parents come from money, actually, though I declined most of it because I didn't want to be the heir to my dad's retail company and forced into his demands for my future. My grandfather left me something, knowing I wanted to be a journalist, so I've been able to take the work I love while still being relatively secure. Something William couldn't have fathomed, I'm sure. But I'm sure Camille could relate."

"Absolutely. For my part, I don't come from much and have always had to sort of scrape by. Our fates are reversed in that way. I guess a sort of balancing."

"But we've both been hyper-aware of economic differences because of the memories, souls, whatever, that chose us. Your essay about the hypocrisy of New York's Nouveau Riche turning their backs on immigrants and the working class they themselves came from was perfection. You're a great writer." When Lillian sat back at this, he chuckled. "Sorry, I had to look you up online after we met."

"No, I did the same thing. You're not so bad yourself. I particularly liked your article about William Randolph Hearst's many sins."

"Man, what an asshole."

"At least we got *Citizen Kane* out of it," Lillian chuckled. "But thank you. I'm glad you liked my work. I'd like to do more."

"You should. Especially about places like this, once vibrant industries now practically a ghost town. There's a lot to ponder."

Nathaniel noted that he'd best get his bag from the Denny bed and breakfast and Lillian waited at the door for him. "If you're not back in two minutes I'm coming in--"

"I don't have much. See you in a minute."

He returned with a small roller bag and his messenger bag, hopping into the car as Lillian directed the driver to next take them up Glazier Drive.

When the car climbed the lane and stopped in the roundabout in front of the Glazier mansion, Bethany came running outside as Nathaniel paid the driver. Exiting, waiting until Nathaniel could stand next to her, Lillian began introducing everyone as the car drove off.

"Nathaniel, this is Bethany Glazier, Bethany, this is Nathaniel Lynd. We had a *really* weird day. Like every other day I've had in this town so far."

"I heard sirens and then saw flashing lights and an ambulance over at the Denny mansion, are you both ok? It tried calling but you didn't pick up."

Lillian shook her head. "I've no idea what happened to my phone in the chaos, sorry."

Bethany took a good look at Nathaniel. "You do look *exactly* like the ghost in my house, Lillian did not lie. That is *weird*."

Nathaniel shrugged. "It gets weirder." He explained what happened.

Bethany scratched her head. "So… a demon-kind-of-ghost, who *another* ghost is saying is Eustus Denny, took over that poor director, and you both got attacked?"

"Yeah. And if you see me wearing a… well, suit of silver armor, I'm just being cautious," Nathaniel chuckled nervously. "I read in the archives over there that Eustus Denny was deathly allergic to silver. So, I'm just not going to take any chances."

"That's weird." Bethany gestured them over to the front foyer. "I never understood this, but… I remember once hearing that my great grandmother was really insistent about this one particular quirk." She shut one of the shutters on the sidelight windows of the door, lifting the lever on the pane to entirely close the blinds. The wood that was dark wood on one interior side was bright silver on the other exterior side if shut entirely. "Paint with real silver in it. It's on every window and door. Carriage house too, if you noticed it."

Lillian ran a hand over her face. "Was he like, a vampire or something? Don't tell me he was a vampire; I know I'm goth but I'm not into *every* trope. I don't think I can handle vampires right now."

Bethany shrugged. "Isn't silver a werewolf thing? I mean, we're all figuring this out as we go along."

Nathaniel sighed. "Couldn't they have left us a guidebook?"

"Maybe they did." Bethany shrugged. "The whole publishing house. *The Curse* was just one of them. Maybe everything in the catalogue is a clue."

Lillian shook her head. "We've got our work cut out for us."

They ordered dinner and devoured it. Lillian was glad to hear Bethany's updates about the other women writers among their team who had each decided to return home but had all agreed to return as soon as funding could be restored.

"I promise I still have a separate account by which to pay you, Lillian, for your archival work. And you, Nathaniel. You've gotten wrapped up in a real-life ghost story of your own. Will we be seeing more of you or has this town made you run screaming?"

"Oh, I'll be here for a little while." He put his hand on the small of Lillian's back, causing a shudder of delight to race up her spine. "I've got a lot of work I can do here. I'm not scared off so easily."

"That's the spirit. As you're an author, and I'm trying to resurrect a publishing house, I hope you'll write something for us."

"I never say no to a new editorial contact, Miss Glazier."

"Call me Bethany. And good, glad to have you in the contact list. Do you need a place to stay tonight, Nathaniel? I mean, I'd be reluctant to stay on Denny land if I were you. And I've got room." She gestured all around her.

"The carriage house is fine," Lillian and Nathaniel said at the same time.

Bethany smirked. "Ok. Suit yourselves."

"But there is something about being here, and in the carriage house, that feels more secure than anywhere else." Lillian said, sharing with Bethany what John the bartender had said about conditional haunting; that they would be seen as proxy family and have a different experience in this place than someone else.

"Yes, I think that must be true. Oh! That reminds me. I was looking through the old silver mine accounts, because that's where the first seed money for the publishing company came from." Bethany went to a stack of papers and thin volumes sitting further down the table and returned with a ledger. "Look at this line item in the Glazier Mine financial records."

Lillian squinted at the tight, looping script and read: "Gift to W and C for elopement & security in New York or Chicago."

"The Glaziers were going to help William and Camille?" Nathaniel asked. "The date correlates with the dates of the newspaper articles written speculating about them, at least, by the year. Camille didn't fall and die until months after this."

"So that feeling of protection likely comes from that sense of familial regard held then," Bethany stated. "That they would offer so much, in the currency of the time, to a staff member and someone from a rival family, it's interesting."

"It is. But we can't just stay on this plot forever," Lillian conceded.

"The Denny mansion, however, is out to get us. Specifically, Nathaniel."

"We'll find ways to fight this," Nathaniel encouraged. "The more we learn about the families, the staff, everyone involved, we'll continue to gain a larger piece of the puzzle."

"Like Matilda Hart," Lillian continued. "Like whoever wanted to help William and Camille leave."

"In some ways," Nathaniel murmured thoughtfully, "our souls persisting, to this day, to tell the tale and reconnect with one another might be part of the battle." His demeanor was as earnest and as hopeful as William's echo.

Lillian nodded.

As they said goodnight to Bethany at the door, she reminded them to use the shutters, even if it was just superstition. "Can't hurt anything," she added.

"I won't argue that," Nathaniel stated. "Thanks, Bethany. I'm glad to know you and despite everything, I'm so glad to have come to this town."

"Me too," Lillian added.

Bethany smiled. "I'm grateful for your friendship and support. Both of you. I bet we can all turn the tide. Hopeful eye forward, careful eye to the past."

"There's a sentence for your publishing mission statement!" Lillian exclaimed.

Turning, she walked towards the carriage house, Nathaniel following.

Once inside and the door locked, Nathaniel pulled her into a warm, tight embrace. "Thank you for coming to rescue me, my damsel in shining armor!"

"I had to save my knight in shining distress from the tower!"

"I suppose I was Sleeping Beauty, wasn't I?" He closed his eyes. "Kiss me and break my spell!"

Giggling, she kissed him, and he reciprocated sensuously. After a moment, Lillian drew back. "Shutters! Let's not get too distracted just yet."

Each going to a different window, they closed every shutter and adjusted the metallically coated slats so that they were closed, silver side out. Once the precautions were complete, they jointly lit a fire in the enormous fireplace. Lillian discovered a bottle of red wine in a kitchen cabinet and opened it for them both, bringing glasses to the fire.

"To us," they toasted. "Whatever that means."

"So, Eustus Denny," Lillian pondered, "the man who was cruel—we know this from how he treated Camille—either had or developed a silver allergy during his lifetime, ironic considering his wealth came from turning mined silver into finery. All when he could have most certainly afforded *not* to be cruel but generous. What, then, turned him into not just a spirit, but a sort of demonic entity? Matilda Hart's ghost seemed to think it was his hatred and violence."

"I'm thinking, if I were to translate that grimoire of his more in-depth, that he made a literal deal with the devil to increase his wealth."

"Well, then…" Lillian went to a drawstring pouch of jewelry and pulled out a pointy silver cross with an anatomical heart made of rubies and draped it over her neck. She pulled out an additional silver chain and clasped it around Nathaniel's neck, clasping a silver bracelet around his wrist, then one on hers.

"Thank you! Gothic armor for the win," he declared, pulling Lillian into his arms. "Now then. We have been rudely interrupted in our amorous exchanges for, what, a hundred and fifty years? I would very much like to make up for some of that lost time. And take my *meticulous* time doing so. Would that be amenable to you, Miss Anders?"

"It very much would, Mister Lynd," she replied, her hand on the buttons of his shirt.

Their kisses were immediate and thorough, as were their explorations. They kept on all the silver, but not much else.

At some point, amidst particularly heated touches, Lillian paused a moment. "Did you hear that?"

"Wind in the trees?"

"No… something shuffling."

It had started as a scrape. A drag and scrape, like a limping set of footsteps. Faint, but definitely approaching.

"That's… unsettling," Nathaniel said, trying to stay calm.

"Terrifying. You mean terrifying." Lillian shook. Nathaniel held her close.

There was a long moment of silence. Even the night creatures that made sounds in the forest had entirely gone quiet. That, perhaps, was the most unsettling of all, as if whatever was coming made nature second-guess itself.

Then a fingernail scratch outside. Across the glass of the windows. A tap. A dragging squeak. A tap. It encircled the entire carriage house. Dragging on glass, stone, timber. They could see nothing, as everything was battened down. But hearing it was enough. Nathaniel and Lillian clutched one another. As the sound traveled, suddenly Nathaniel jumped up and went to the dining table, grabbing the silver candelabras on the runner.

He ran to set one candelabra at the base of the front door, the other at the back, just as the sound was scraping its way towards the rear exit. Lillian jumped up and went to the silverware drawer, placing a fork, spoon or knife at every sill or threshold.

The sound faded.

Lillian thought of Sally's video. "We *have* to figure out how to get that thing back inside that silver box again. Until we do, it's always going to sniff around for us."

"We'll keep looking. For now, let's just enjoy one another's company. It, in and of itself, is an act of resistance."

They sealed their refusal to be terrorized with a kiss and continued expressing newfound passions.

Chapter Eleven

A BLARING SOUND WOKE LILLIAN. A phone, ringing. It wasn't hers—that was still lost somewhere. The ring was loud and jarring.

With everything shut, she had no idea what time it was, but cracks of bright sunlight were coming in through the tiny slits in the shutters.

Nathaniel stirred beside her, the covers all tangled from their amorous explorations. Bleary-eyed, she found herself blissful at the sight of him, her heart soaring. Only after acknowledging the thrill of him next to her did she remember the terrifying sounds that had patrolled outside.

She threw her robe on and padded out into the center room. The ringing was coming from the kitchen area, where an old rotary phone hung on the wall by the refrigerator. She picked up with a hesitant hello.

"Hi Lillian, it's Bethany. Since you didn't have your phone, I had to use the old landline. The Guidanos are here. Melody's in her vestments. I... think they want to do some kind of exorcism? You might want to talk to them."

"Oh... ok... give me a... minute."

"Yeah, I'll stall them while you get dressed," Bethany said knowingly and hung up.

Lillian turned to the coffee pot and hit the brew button.

"Thank you for your coffee prioritization," Nathaniel called after her.

"Creatures of the night need extra help rising from their coffins," Lillian said, returning to the bedroom and trying to put her hair up into something that didn't look like she'd been mauled.

"I could make some kind of innuendo about you getting a *rise* out of me, but I'll just say instead, good morning, Lillian, it is a gift to be next to you. Last night was... Everything."

"Why thank you, Nathaniel, the feeling is *quite* mutual." She leaned over and kissed him. "Get dressed. I think we've got to go do an exorcism."

He stared at her for a moment, then nodded. "As one does."

Rummaging in his bag, he pulled out a unique charcoal button-down shirt with velvet flocking in dark stripes, and a different vest, this one in a deep red. The fact that they both had a clear style, neither very 'modern,' both certainly informed by fashion of the past, felt like another piece of the puzzle that fit just so.

Lillian slipped into a black lace blouse and peasant skirt with black lace gathers, making sure the cross and all the silver trappings were visible outside the layers. Nathaniel pulled out the pendant she'd given him from against his skin to be displayed outside his shirt.

"Before we go..." Nathaniel swept her into his arms for a soft kiss. "I don't know if I was clear enough last night. Yes, memories of William and Camille's exploits inspire me, but it's *you* I'm here for."

She returned the kiss fully. "You are the most delightful thing that's ever happened to me. And I want to keep exploring what that means, without fear. Which is why we have to get the evil that still wants to keep us apart under control."

Exiting the carriage house with travel coffee cups in hand, Lillian noticed Carmen Guidano chatting with Bethany under the portico of the mansion, a bandage on her forehead. Beside Carmen stood a woman in a white clerical robe and purple stole.

"The lovebirds have awoken from their nest," Bethany announced. Carmen turned to them sheepishly.

The woman in vestments was likely in her fifties or so, around Carmen's age, bright-eyed and round-cheeked, with spiky white hair that had a streak dyed pink on either side. She strode up to Lillian and Nathaniel and shook their hands enthusiastically. A huge silver cross hung around her neck and her purple stole was decorated with stylized, embroidered doves.

"Hello, I'm Melody. Rev Mel if you feel the need to use a title, it's nice to meet you. Sorry you had a *hell* of a day yesterday. No thanks to my wife." Reverend Mel elbowed Carmen, who flushed with shame.

"I'm so sorry," Carmen said, tears in her eyes.

"It's ok. Something came over you," Nathaniel offered. "Literally."

"We all saw it," Lillian said, empathetically. "Including some trapped spirit of William Hart's aunt who managed to help, too." She laughed mordantly. "There was a lot going on."

Carmen stared at Nathaniel with a disappointed teacher's expression. "You went into the room I told you not to go in, didn't you?"

Nathaniel put his arms up. "I did. Guilty as charged, and Lillian has reminded me that doing so triggered part of the curse. But to my credit, I did not take the spooky book out of the spooky box. That was already out on the desk. *With* dust on it. Someone else let something loose."

"Sally, the woman taking video. She's who let the shadow out," Lillian explained. "She livestreamed it on her channel."

Carmen sighed angrily. "I *told* her not to go in there--"

"Yeah, you can't tell them anything. Cindy died in the mine," Bethany said through clenched teeth. "You'd think Sally would know better."

"Well," Melody clapped her hands. "Let's cleanse the house, then. I mean, I'd rather burn it down, but it *is* a landmark and Carmen wouldn't let me anyway." She turned to Lillian and Nathaniel. "I mean, you don't have to come. I wouldn't blame you if *you* burned the house down, but I wanted to extend the invitation to join us for a bit of closure."

"Cleansing the house is a good idea," Nathaniel said, gesturing they move ahead.

Lillian followed reluctantly. "How about exorcisms, you good with those?"

"Only in a pinch," Melody laughed.

"It needs one," Lillian insisted.

"I *told* you," Carmen said. "It needs something stronger than just a house blessing."

"Then we give the place what it needs," the pastor declared with a smile that was absolutely contagious. Her good cheer might do half the exorcism rite in and of itself. She turned to her wife. "It isn't that I didn't believe you, my dear. I knew you'd never harm anyone of your own volition, I just didn't want to scare my new friends by bringing the powers and principalities of evil and darkness into the mix when they're so new in town."

"We saw the entity ourselves. At least, I did," Lillian shared. "So please don't hesitate to tell us the truth about things. We need to know, for our safety."

They had begun walking down the slope when Carmen turned to Bethany. "You're coming too?"

Bethany nodded. "I need to know everything I can about what's going on here. Sort of a liability thing. The more information my lawyers have about all the threats, the better protected the publishing house will be. Plus, if I can learn how to protect my *friends*, that's the more important thing."

Lillian smiled at her. "That's really nice and brave of you. But— and please don't take this the wrong way—I wonder if your presence, as a Glazier descendant, might not be welcome? I'd hate for the place to be additionally unsafe for you. In the way that we were more protected in the Glazier property, you might be all the more vulnerable in a Denny home. This particular vendetta from the past doesn't have to do with you, not directly, and I'd love to not put you in danger."

Bethany swallowed hard. "I'm sorry if I seem scared and you're trying to let me off the hook--"

"No, you're great, we're all scared," Lillian reassured. "I just don't know how this is going to go and it might be better if you literally held down the Glazier fort and called in emergency services if you don't hear from us later on in the day."

Lillian sighed, trying to source the particular point of bone-deep panic that had welled up in her when Bethany said she wanted to join them. "I'm not trying to give orders here. I think, to be honest, Camille really doesn't want anyone else to get hurt on her account. I can't always feel her, exactly, but I do now. The Glaziers did a lot to try to shield and protect her and William, and she doesn't want Eustus' anger to get taken out on you. I'm not sure the demon he's become is aware it isn't still the 19th century."

Melody seemed a bit confused but didn't interject. Carmen just seemed worried.

Bethany nodded. "I'll be in the mansion, then. Armed with a silver mug of coffee. And maybe a knife. Call me, any of you, if you need anything. *Anything*." She hugged Lillian. Then, in an awkward moment of sentiment, hastily hugged Nathaniel, Carmen and Melody. "Go with whatever God, or none, sustains you."

The party separated and the four plodded down the curving slope, the Denny mansion coming into view in the distance. Just the sight of the building made Lillian shudder. Nathaniel noticed and grabbed her hand. She was determined to bolster herself with camaraderie instead of dread. She turned to the clergywoman. "How did you and Carmen meet, Rev Mel?"

"Catholic school," Melody and Carmen chorused and laughed. "We got expelled when Reverend Mother found us kissing behind the grotto," Melody continued, as gleeful as if it had been just yesterday. "Her face, it was so red. I'd wanted to be a nun myself, but, well, Carmen changed that, so I went to seminary. Being clergy is more comprehensive anyway and the Episcopalians took me on. It was still a fight for us, back then, I won't lie, but the church got right with us in time. Love and faith are worth fighting for, aren't they?"

Lillian and Nathaniel glanced at one another and smiled. Whatever was left of Camille rallied like a soldier given a speech by a commanding officer.

"What about you?" Melody asked, gesturing at Lillian and Nathaniel. "Did you come to town together?"

"No, we're reincarnate lost lovers from the mid-1800s who just found each other again," Lillian replied. Nathaniel raised his eyebrows at her. "What? That's hardly the most absurd thing anyone has said or experienced lately, seeing as we're en route to an exorcism. We need to be honest about our 'fore-selves' part in this. It will get dragged in." Lillian addressed Melody and explained further. "That's what I was talking about with Bethany. I've inherited some of Camille Denny's memories while Nathaniel has taken on William Hart. All of it sort of 'woke up' when we came here."

Melody turned to Carmen, who just shrugged. "This town is weird,

Mel. *You're* the one that answered the call at All Souls. I just followed, don't blame me."

Chuckling, Melody turned back to Lillian, gesturing to the cross with the ruby heart on it. "Just so I know what's what, is that a symbol of faith or just a goth thing?"

"Uh, just a goth thing, sorry. I've never known what to believe. We're wearing silver because Nathaniel read that Eustus Denny had a severe silver allergy and there must be something to it because Bethany's ancestors painted all the shutters silver."

Melody nodded thoughtfully. "I *did* think that was a peculiar design choice, those reflective shutters. As for not knowing what to believe, we're all on a journey, let's just try to be kind to one another as we fumble around."

"That's theology I can get behind," Nathaniel stated.

They stood staring at the Denny mansion, hesitating outside. Lillian's eyes fell again on the windowsill with its long, claw-like soot marks. "What started the fire in the seventies?"

"From what I've been told," Carmen began with a sigh, shifting on her feet on the stoop, "the fire department couldn't determine the source. Trespassers had broken in and conducted a séance. Of course, that was during a wave of 'satanic panic', so everyone assumed they were some sort of sacrificial cult when they were just bored teens exploring a house they'd been told was haunted. I talked to one of them about it, as they're now a major donor to the historical society. They said they were on the second floor when something rushed past them and out the window, towards the Glazier mansion, an odd-looking fire in its wake, like no fire they'd ever seen. The teens all scattered but one managed to call the fire department. Several people died in town that day, all from heart attacks or falls. The fire was contained and the structure itself was stable enough to stand. The next week, a Denny descendant returned to town with a silver box and locked up the study. The house sat empty again for another ten years before it opened as the historical society."

"Do you have a fire extinguisher in the house?" Lillian asked.

Carmen nodded. "A small one in every room." She turned apologetically to Nathaniel. "If you'd rather I stay outside, I understand--"

"No," Nathaniel shook his head. "You were attacked too, manipulated, hurt. This is for all of us."

Lillian squared her shoulders, stepping up to the front door. "Camille has to make peace with this building. She was imprisoned in it and died falling from it. I don't want it to have a hold on her, or me, anymore."

Carmen nodded, fighting back tears. "If it helps you feel safer, Nathaniel, I poured out everything that had been in the mansion's historical medicine cabinet that we had on display. I didn't know any of those bottles had anything in them. Unfortunately, Eustus did. I wish, during that 'possession' I'd glimpsed more of an understanding of how to stop him, but I was entirely overtaken. There wasn't any nuance, just hatred. I tried fighting…"

"We know, we saw," Lillian said, placing a hand on her shoulder. "If you hadn't fought, we *all* could have died."

"Let's keep fighting, my dears," Melody said gently, the first to actually step inside once Carmen unlocked the door, entering with cross raised in her hand. "I'm wearing silver, love, as are our friends, do grab a candlestick on your way in?"

In the entrance hall, Carmen removed a taper from a silver candlestick on a narrow entrance foyer table and tucked the hefty holder under her arm.

The group followed the Reverend as she went room to room to do a blessing in each, pulling out a silver dispenser of holy water that spritzed each room. Pulling out a small prayerbook from a vestment pocket, she opened it at the ribbon placeholder and began reciting a blessing. Everyone recited back a prayer when she nodded at them to respond communally. Perhaps it was just Lillian's imagination, but the energy of the house seemed to lighten and lift as they went.

Going upstairs, hesitating outside the door to Eustus' study, Carmen posed a shaky question. "Is there a way to summon that thing back, without it taking over anyone, to put it back where it came from?"

"Well," Nathaniel began carefully. "We know what made Eustus Denny the angriest he'd ever been in life…"

Suddenly, he went down on one knee and turned to Lillian, proffering the small simple band he wrested from his pinky finger, lifting it up to her. "I, William Hart, ask you, Camille Denny, love of my life, to marry me. Will you marry me?"

Lillian felt the room spin. "Um…"

Nathaniel leaned towards her with a whisper. "We're trying to draw out angry old Eustus who *hated* their relationship to the point of death… This might do it, if we play the parts…"

Lillian's face went bright red as she chuckled uneasily. "Right." She straightened her shoulders and responded to the proposal in a loud, stilted tone. "Yes. Yes! I, Camille Denny, will marry you, William Hart! Love of my life!"

Nathaniel stood again and kissed her dramatically at the open door. "Now, we are betrothed!" He announced theatrically.

A terrible growl sounded, as if coming up from the bowels of hell and all the lights in the building went out at once.

Lillian screamed. Nathaniel held her protectively.

The backup generator kicked on, offering a flickering, jaundiced and eerie light. There were no windows in Eustus' study and only one back-up light, a long and unsteady fluorescent bulb over top of one of the bookshelves, casting the room partly in a grim, blinking light, partly in shadow.

"It's here," Carmen murmured, frightened, glancing at the deep shadows of the windowless hallway and room. Melody moved in front of her wife, one hand lifting her silver dispenser of holy water, the other lifting her Episcopalian prayer book.

Nathaniel dragged Lillian into the study itself, standing before an open book on the desk, next to the open silver box.

"I'm not letting this thing frighten me," he said, kissing her again.

She gave into the kiss and joined in his strength of conviction. "And we're not letting it win," she murmured against him, feeling righteous anger swell within her like a match catching tinder.

In the reflection cast by a glass bookcase, Lillian saw the two of them reflected in 19th century clothes again. This time, her image captured the gown Camille was imprisoned—and died—in. This was Camille's final stand.

"Do you hear them? We're not going to give up," Camille stated from the reflection defiantly, staring at something just behind Nathaniel and pointing so that Lillian would see it. Instinctively, Lillian lifted the silver pendant around her neck and shoved Nathaniel to the side, trying to get him out of harm's way as something large and terrible swooped at them.

Lillian felt claws strike her shoulder, as if trying to rip at her necklace but was repelled by it and the claw landed to the side, tearing at her sleeve. She cried out, slapping a hand to her shoulder blade and when she drew it away, her palm was slick with a bloody sheen. Nathaniel reached for her and as he did, she noticed he'd sustained a scratch across his face. The claws of the enemy were long and cut a wide swath.

Rev Mel began reciting scripture in a firm, strong voice, offering renunciations of evil that Lillian recognized from her admittedly limited understanding of actual exorcisms—though *The Exorcist* was one of her favorite films—and the entity snarled. The shadows coalesced into a figure that retreated on haunches, a darkened mass of bitterness and rot with glimmering eyes that were the stuff of nightmare.

Nathaniel was still holding Lillian, though they shifted in each other's hold, as if trying to alternately shield the other in an awkward, embracing dance.

Nathaniel pointed down to the open book he'd described to her as Eustus' grimoire. "I think *this* is key," he stated. Picking it up, the creature snarled again at Nathaniel's actions. It tried to pounce but was held back by Melody reading another line of renunciations in the name of God and saints, holding out her silver cross.

Nathaniel read a line of Latin from Eustus' 'book of shadows.' To Lillian's surprise and delight, he read the language smoothly. Expertly. At this, the skeletal shadow roared, floating above the book.

The entity plunged claws down against Lillian and Nathaniel's heads as if trying to anchor itself to them. A gruesome, knife's point dug into their temples in a blinding, searing agony.

Scenes flashed through Lillian's mind, Camille's endless fight with a man who had never shown love, only control, worsening after her mother died, and it warped him into a monster long before his spirit had ever become one.

"You'll never escape me." Eustus Denny growled in the past, to Camille, and in the present to Lillian, an echoing threat from an amorphous, sagging mouth that stank of sulphur and death.

The demonic force was the most horrifying, insidious thing and while Lillian was rightly terrified of the creature that was trying to rip her apart, the righteous anger she'd been cultivating all her life—from the moment she first learned about the historical and broad limitations on women's autonomy to the specific injustices of Camille's imprisonment—roared forth.

"We already did escape you!" Camille and Lillian shrieked as one. "We've returned! *You're* the one who is going away. You've no power over us! Not then, not now! You may have tried to stop my heart, but you'll never stop my spirit, no matter where it lands!"

Blood trickling down the side of her face, Lillian turned to Nathaniel, even though moving was agony and drove the claw further down her cheek. "Keep reading! Trap this demon and *end* this."

Nathaniel, fighting the agony he was subjected to in turn, read another line of Latin. In doing so, the shadow seemed to wriggle and flail, visibly tethered to the book, as if Nathaniel had caught the dread shadow like a fish on a hook. Melody kept reciting scripture, coming closer and reaching out her cross towards the roiling mist of the shadow which undulated and tried to evade any touch of silver, edging it closer to the book reeling it in.

Noting that his efforts had a specific effect, Nathaniel re-read the last line and continued onto the next. Lillian had no idea what Nathaniel was saying, only that he read without a hitch.

After another struggle, the shadow tried to move its claws like a knife through their bodies. The creature roared and from within the center of the insidious mass, an odd yellow spark of a flame snapped to life and began widening out in a gaseous fireball. Nathaniel and Lillian began coughing from the noxious stench.

Melody's scripture recitations seemed to still the path of the demon's hooks, freezing its claws in place, though blood now streamed down the side of Lillian and Nathaniel's faces and onto their necks and shoulders.

The lights flickered frenetically, and the ground trembled beneath them. The edges of the grimoire started to smoke. Nathaniel hissed in pain. Carmen came in with a cry, a small fire extinguisher in hand, covering them all in a light layer of foam, the spray glancing off the demon in gritty drops.

Nathaniel shouted another line in Latin. After a harrowing, ear-splitting howl, at long last the shadow was pulled into the book.

Slamming the book closed, Nathaniel shoved it in the silver box.

Melody ran over, yanking the cross off from around her neck, part of her silver chain flying, and shoved the cross onto the top of the book, where it shuddered violently.

Lillian shut the silver box and latched the long bolts across its seam.

Nathaniel drew back, waving his hands, his palms red from slight burns, shaking off the foam.

Melody continued with a benediction as the lights returned to normal. Carmen crossed herself and came over to tend to Lillian and Nathaniel's wounds. They hissed in turn as alcohol swabs were pressed against each slice and puncture, and she carefully set small bandages across each. Gently, she used additional swabs to remove the bulk of the gore from their necks and shoulders and helped dust off some of the remaining extinguisher foam. "Sorry, you're going to have to wash these clothes and hope it comes out, there's a lot of blood and debris in the fibers."

"Thank you," Lillian said, rallying a wan smile. "Advantage of always wearing black, hides the bloodstains."

"I think the worst of it is over?" Nathaniel said hopefully.

"I hope so," Lillian replied, reaching out and caressing his arm fondly. "What did you recite and how did you know to recite it? Great work, by the way."

"I double majored in history and Latin in college. Dad laughed at me, but I insisted. I had the odd feeling it would come in handy someday. William likely looking out for me this whole time. The book said something about putting something back that had been opened, so I said it. And we put something back and closed it."

"I hope it's that simple," Carmen said wearily. "But I don't want that thing to stay up here. Come. Let's shut this all up until we figure out what to do." Shuddering, Carmen beckoned them all into the hall and closed the study door behind her, swiftly locking it. "I didn't realize anything was *in* that box or that it was a danger. I thought it was just decorative and I was obliging Eustus' great grandson. He'd come by when I first took the job, asking that everything be kept in that study as it had been in life."

"I think we should bury the box," Lillian stated.

"Cement it over, *then* bury it," Nathaniel added.

"In the silver mine," Melody chimed in.

"*Carefully* in the silver mine if there's any safe access," Lillian cautioned. "Remember, a woman just died in there."

"Was it Eustus' spirit that did that, do you think?" Carmen asked ruefully.

Lillian shook her head. "No, I saw the footage, unfortunately. There was no shadow. No hands. No claws. Nothing visible like we saw in there." Lillian gestured towards the study. "In the mine, she died by an unseen shove. It must have been the *curse* that did that to her. Eustus' spirit could never have withstood the traces of silver all around. Bethany Glazier specifically told us to not go anywhere in the mansion or mine that had been marked restricted. The curse that was levied *after* Camille and William's death follows those who don't listen to warnings, with a particular bias for *Glazier* family warnings."

"But I'm sure it's like what John at The Blue Taper said," Nathaniel offered. "Saying that 'curse' could be generally applied in this town, depending on your experience. You could either do something to be provocative, in the case of Cindy, or potentially get caught in the crosshairs of another person's sniping. I think there's a great deal to understand in this place, and I'm interested in taking the time to do it."

An idea struck Lillian. "I know where to take the box. I'm sorry, Carmen, can I go into the study again? I'm going to take it."

Carmen hesitated a moment, then sighed and obliged. Lillian entered the room, looking around warily. Nathaniel was right behind her, as if he didn't dare let her get far. Reassured that nothing else was lurking in any shadow or ready to pounce, Lillian strode to the desk and picked up the silver box.

It was much heavier than it looked but she didn't strain, strengthened by a fire of purpose and a very old rage that was finally flexing its muscles of justice.

As she and Nathaniel rejoined Carmen and Melody in the hallway,

Lillian saw Camille reflected again, this time in the oval mirror at the center of the hall.

"Do you want me to carry--" Nathaniel reached for the box.

"No," Lillian said fiercely. Camille's nostrils flared in the reflection, rage illuminating her visage. Words that weren't entirely Lillian's burst from her lips. "Father imprisoned me and left me to die. It's only fair to return the favor. For the safety of everyone."

Melody and Carmen stepped back, surprised by this ferocious channeling, while Nathaniel stepped closer, drawn in. His reflection could be seen as William in the glass, staring down at Camille lovingly. "Of course, my darling," he said reverently, his voice his own and yet not. "Your will reigns."

Carmen locked the study door behind them again. Lillian felt like she was leading a funeral processional out of the building with the way she was carrying the box. She paused halfway down the stoop, waiting for everyone else to exit.

Flipping the *closed* sign over the Historical Society door, Carmen turned to her wife at the top of the steps. "Mel, what about taking that vacation we've been talking about for years?"

"Thought you'd never ask!" Melody crowed.

Lillian turned to look back up at Melody. "Thank you, we couldn't have contained that thing without you." She turned to Carmen. "And thank you for taking care of us."

"Least we could do. You did very well, the two of you. Braver than I could have been."

"I didn't really feel I had a choice," Lillian said. "And I suppose that's a good thing." Nathaniel nodded agreement.

"Do you want us to come with you?" Carmen asked, pointing to the box.

"No," Lillian insisted. "Camille *really* wants to be the one to see this through."

"If anything goes sideways, we'll call for backup," Nathaniel added.

"May you find the closure you seek, dear souls," Melody offered a final benediction as they crossed to Glazier's Drive.

Chapter Twelve

AS LILLIAN AND NATHANIEL BEGAN the winding climb towards the mine, at the foot of Glazier Drive, something reflective glimmered at the crossroad.

"And there's my phone," Lillian said with a small laugh, setting down the silver box, kneeling to examine the damage to her phone. When she picked up the device only a few scrapes the worse for wear, a rock beside where it had landed caught her eye. Carved into the glittering gray stone was a heart, a W and a C. Camille remembered using a hairpin to etch the mark and tie a love note to it before throwing it down to her waiting sweetheart standing at the crossroad.

"Oh my God..." Nathaniel said, staring at the stone. William must have recognized it too.

Ceremoniously, Lillian kissed the relic of their hard-fought love and set the stone atop the silver box. She rose and continued walking.

Lillian didn't realize how lost in thought she was until Nathaniel asked a question.

"So. Can I ask where we are heading with the box of doom and that unexpected souvenir?"

"Oh, sorry. There's a winding, stone stair to the side of the mine where it opens up to a forest clearing above. I think somewhere up there we can find a crevice to bury this in. I just have a hunch about it, and at this point, I think we should be trusting any strong instincts we have."

"Absolutely. Lead the way."

They fell to silence again and Lillian didn't realize how deeply Camille's memories had recaptured her. The ferocity with which she'd burst forth, likely drawn further out by those demonic claws trying to snuff her out, yet again, remained as a loud hum in Lillian's mind and ears. Camille had been so sick at the end of her life; she'd not been healthy enough to be properly furious about how she'd been treated; no better than a trapped animal in a cold cage. But she'd had so much to be angry about. Lillian felt like she could scream and cause another avalanche if she wasn't careful; a past life made into a present banshee.

Also, it troubled her, thinking about how the book and the box had been separate entities. Something didn't quite add up.

After another few moments, Nathaniel continued. "I'm admittedly very new at reading your expressions, Lillian, but it seems like you're trying to figure something out. If you don't want to say a word, that's fine, please tell me to shut up, but if you'd like to problem-solve with me—"

"I'm trying to understand what happened in the seventies during the fire, when Eustus may have 'gotten out' *then*. I can't imagine those sooty claw marks on the sill are from anything but him. Who put him back in, then, for his shadow to then have been released *again* by Sally? You said the book—his grimoire—was already out of the box and on the desk when you arrived yesterday. So, he got put back in the box but not back in the book?"

"*Now* that polaroid in the study makes sense," Nathaniel exclaimed. "In all the chaos of everything, it's a detail I forgot to mention. On a shelf behind the desk, I noticed a polaroid of a priest holding a cross over the silver box. It was dated 1979. In that photo, the grimoire was *out*, sitting beside the silver box, on the desk. I made special note of it, to see if the arrangement of the desk was the same as it had been then. It was. Somehow, that priest must have contained the entity to the box but not understood or been able to additionally trap it inside the book."

A flutter of the curtains in the parlor window of the Glazier mansion must have meant Bethany had seen or heard them. In a few moments she rushed out.

"You're ok!" She exclaimed, looking them up and down. "Bandaged, and… bloodied, I see, but ok otherwise?"

"Yes. We made it," Lillian said triumphantly.

"What happened?!"

Lillian set the box down on the ground and put a foot on it as she and Nathaniel explained as many details about what had happened as they could remember.

Bethany appeared overwhelmed. "Wow. This is *not* what I signed up for in re-opening this publishing house."

"Probably a lot of the original authors felt the same way," Lillian said. She thought how sad it was that *The Curse* was the last thing poor Martha Green ever wrote.

"I still need help if you're game to keep going," Bethany said sheepishly. "There's enough paperwork to employ both of you if you've got time in your schedule. But I also understand if you've had enough of this place, especially after this. I feel like I've been saying that a lot, trying to apologize—"

"You've nothing to apologize for and I think I'm in a bit too deep now to run," Lillian replied. "I mean, now that I'm engaged and all," she laughed, elbowing Nathaniel, who grinned at her.

"Really?" Bethany was shocked. "I mean, congrats, but you've only known each other, what—"

"No, for *pretend*," Lillian laughed. "It was pretty smart of Nathaniel, to fake a proposal to bring forth the angry, demonic remains of Eustus Denny. He certainly came roaring back to try to stop us." She put a hand to her bandaged head. "But anyway…" She chuckled nervously, feeling her cheeks flush with heat. She took a moment to remove the silver band from her finger and hand it back to him. "Here."

"Keep it. Please," Nathaniel said softly. "Looks good on you."

She stared at him and was moved, exited and instantly desirous, glancing at the carriage house and what delights could await them.

Bethany cleared her throat, suddenly a very obvious third wheel. "So, are you hungry? Does exorcism work up an appetite? Can I order in some sushi? Pizza?"

"Yes," they chorused.

"Ok, sushi and pizza it is!" Bethany exclaimed, gesturing them inside.

Lillian picked up the box again. "*After* we bury this damnable box in the mine."

Bethany held up her hands. "Wait, no. I'm sorry, *no one* is going back in the mine--"

"Not in it, *against* it," Lillian clarified. "I've an idea, up the staircase to the clearing above. He'll be surrounded by silver."

Bethany nodded, heading to her door. "All right, just come in when you're finished. Take care," she said, clearly uneasy. "You sure you'll be ok?"

"Camille needs this," Lillian said firmly. Bethany nodded and disappeared into the mansion's shadows. "Follow me," she said to Nathaniel. He did without question.

At the back of the carriage house, continuing the curving slope up Glazier Drive, Lillian grabbed a gardening trowel from a potting station on the tiled back patio, placed it atop the silver box beside the carved stone and kept walking.

This time the silence between them held.

A few blackbirds squawked in the trees overhead.

Lillian felt everything that Camille had struggled with during her young life; fury, terror, pain, exhaustion and the unbearable heartbreak that the person causing her such agony was someone who should have been a parent, a loved one, not a jailor and torturer. That she held the bitter essence of that tyrant in this box was a powerful emotional knot. Even though the demon was contained, would it still haunt her in tension? In looking over her shoulder or worriedly into every shadow to see if a shape lurked there?

No. She wouldn't let it. One could live in fear, or one could live into possibility.

She glanced at Nathaniel, who was looking around at the woods as they climbed the curving stone stair, staring as if in recognition. Perhaps he was awash in William's thoughts and emotions too, pulled between their past and this present.

133

"Did you notice that every street and path in this town is on a curve?" Lillian asked quietly. "Everything has a slope and a winding arc."

"I did notice. It's disorienting. But I'd like to think it bends me closer to discoveries. To new opportunities. To you." He leaned towards her and kissed her cheek. Clearly, he was also making the choice to set aside worry for something more hopeful.

As they stepped up into the clearing, the air shimmered before them and William's echo came into view, still dressed in his long coat and open shirtsleeves, the disheveled romantic with hair waving gently as if he were underwater. Love shone on his transparent face. The phantasm floated above a patch of jewelweed wildflowers.

Nathaniel rocked back on his heels, startled by the sight of his mirror image. Lillian set the heavy silver box down near the opening of the clearing but kept the carved rock in the palm of her hand.

"Hello, William," Lillian greeted the specter, "I wasn't sure if I would see you again. I'm not sure how any of this works, ghost, echo, soul..."

Nathaniel stared at the apparition then patted himself, as if to see if he were still standing and real.

"You did it," William said to Lillian proudly. "You remembered." Looking between both her and Nathaniel, he shifted his focus to Nathaniel. "And you came. You listened to what was inside. I'm so proud."

"If I'm here, but part of you is powering me, is *in* me... what are you?" Nathaniel asked, pointing between himself and the spirit.

"William and Camille's love was so powerful it created its own ghost to mark the occasion," the echo declared. "My manifestation would serve as an anchor for those who would try to get right what eluded us. If it had been you that had first come to town, Nathaniel, this echo might have appeared to you as Camille, asking you to remember the past and pull Lillian to you like a magnet, drawing her to the here and now."

Nathaniel reached out and ran a hand down Lillian's back. "Drawn like a magnet is no understatement."

"I was so hoping it would be you, Lillian," the spirit said. "I'd tried so hard to make others see, a few who came before you. Martha Green was so close. She had channeled us but couldn't seem to realize us, or the truths that surpassed her writing. She couldn't see or hear me, no matter what I tried. And in the end, that was the death of her. I tried to warn her not to leave Glazier mansion the day of the fire, the day the demon first escaped. I wrote a note in dust because she couldn't see me. But she ran from the house. A heart attack just at the end of Glazier Drive and I could do nothing to stop it. But you. You made it through."

"We did make it through," Lillian said heavily. She held up the carved heart to William's echo, as if to prove their triumph and tears immediately glimmered in his luminous eyes. She pressed the stone to her heart. "And now we have to bury the demon that plagued us all."

William stared at the box on the clearing floor for a long moment. Finally, the echo nodded and pointed to a sloping rise in the clearing. Lillian took the box over to it. There was a small, rectangular grate.

"One of the air shafts of the mine," the spirit explained. "It's blocked on the other end."

Nathaniel pulled the face of the grate off. Lillian set Camille's stone down beside the opening. The blackbirds in the trees grew louder. Looking up, Lillian noticed that they were beginning to swarm. William's echo noticed too. Hastily, Lillian shoved the box in the narrow shaft until it hit dirt a couple of feet in.

Grabbing the trowel, Nathaniel sifted dirt in to bury the gleam of the box. Lillian thought of Poe's burial-by-hand story, "The Cask of Amontillado," and offered a bitter, "Yes, for the love of God!"

The murmuration of blackbirds crested in pitch and Nathaniel looked up in concern.

William's echo bellowed in anger. "We *will* have *peace* in this town, damn you! *Peace and freedom*!" With sheer force of will and fury, the apparition managed to pick up Camille's heart-etched rock and hurl it into the shaft where it clanged against the locked box.

The blackbirds scattered as if the rock had been a gunshot. The sky grew quiet again and the clouds that had begun to darken when Eustus appeared had thinned to a pleasant atmosphere.

Quickly, Nathaniel continued to block the passage with dirt all the way to the surface where he closed the grate over it again. Lillian and Nathaniel turned to the hovering spirit who had grown brighter in his fury but seemed fully satisfied with his final word on the matter.

"There." William smiled. "We'll scatter jewelweed seeds across this rise, and it will be entirely forgotten. No one will disturb this evil."

Lillian brushed dirt off her dress and addressed the floating figure. "Thank you. Can *you* find peace, now? Will you be able to rest?"

"Perhaps I'll fade," the spirit mused. "Perhaps I'll grow stronger because of your reconnection." He looked between the two of them fondly. "It is hard to say. Glazier's Gap has a hard time letting go of things. Often it grasps too tightly, running the risk of stifling it. But I think for me, perhaps I have become an heirloom of this place. And now, a guardian." The spirit gestured towards where they'd buried the entity. "That it—*he*—is imprisoned now is quite the poetic reversal, and I know I'll never tire of it."

"Will we have anything to fear from the remaining Denny family members?" Lillian asked. "Will they go looking for the box?"

"I don't think so," the echo replied. "The remaining descendants want nothing to do with the Historical Society. Illness plagued the whole family, all of them after Camille's death, and for the next generations. Literal 'sins of the father.' The great grandson was the one who made the box, he was particularly sensitive. He sensed Eustus in the building and it took a toll on his health."

"Is he the one that called the priest in in 1979, before the fire?" Nathaniel asked.

"Likely so," the apparition replied.

"Leaving the box there was a danger," Lillian mused.

"Yes, but people do get attached to their ancestors, even bad ones. It was David, this great grandson, who finally gave up on the property, after the fire, convincing the rest of the family they'd all be better off on the West Coast, keeping the three smaller mansions as rental properties and a bed and breakfast."

"And you've watched it all, through the years, waiting?" Nathaniel put a hand to his heart.

"As much as I could. Admittedly, there are places an echo like me can't travel, like into a Denny property. And I haven't wanted to be too intrusive in what needs to be *your* lives. I've been a testament to their love living on, waiting for its second chance. Trying to help it all make sense for whoever took on their mantle."

Lillian and Nathaniel glanced at one another and took hands. "Thank you," Lillian said. "I'll try to do as right by Camille as I know how."

"And I by… you," Nathaniel said. "As *weird* as all this is."

"That's all anyone can ask." The echo smiled. "You've handled all this brilliantly, considering. I hope today's actions can bring peace."

They nodded and the echo faded away. They began to descend back to Glazier Drive again.

"It's so weird to… see a mirror of yourself like that," Nathaniel said. "The reflections, too, part of us and yet not. It's made my head spin."

"Same."

Nathaniel squeezed her hand tightly. "But you make my head spin in a way that's worth all the confusion."

Lillian smiled and brought his hand up to kiss it, still a bit too overwhelmed by the gravity and the terror of the day to know what to say.

"Since I'll be sticking around for a while, provided you still don't mind--"

"I insist."

"I think I'll take Bethany up on her offer of a room in the mansion. I'd like to give you a *bit* of space here while we attempt to explore our lives. And ourselves. Even though I've known you for a lifetime and beyond…"

"The carriage house doors will always be open for you," she said with a smile as they walked past and under the portico of the great Glazier mansion.

They joined Bethany who gestured them eagerly into the dining room.

"I haven't had an appetite until now," Lillian murmured. "But I'm starving. Thank you for this, Bethany."

Dinner in the Glazier dining room was pleasant. They feasted upon cheese pizza and avocado rolls, as promised. Afterwards, Nathaniel gasped in delighted wonder as Bethany gave him the tour of the mansion, Lillian following along. He chose a room at the end of the hall to stay in, with side windows overlooking the carriage house.

"Not," Nathaniel clarified to Lillian, "because I want to spy on you."

137

"No, I know why you picked it," Lillian blurted, memories flashing before her eyes. "Camille stayed here in this room, several times, under the guise of calling on Roberta, the eldest Glazier daughter, who helped William and Camille plot and plan escape. You likely feel this place was a haven, as I did with the carriage house."

"Roberta treated staff like they were her own family," Nathaniel continued. "She'd been the one to arrange the riding lessons for Camille in the first place, and once she saw her with William, she knew it was true love. From then on, she tried to shield them from Camille's increasingly unhinged father."

"After mother died of a fever, he was never the same…" Lillian mourned, in a voice that wasn't entirely her own. "The family rivalry increased exponentially after that."

Coming to, rousing from the memories, Lillian turned to Bethany. "Sorry, I'm sure this all sounds wild, but I've been very overwhelmed, being here, with memories and old sentiments and things I know without knowing how I know them. It just all comes tumbling out. Very 'unreliable narrator' of me."

Bethany shook her head. "It's fascinating. I'm glad to learn and be witness to it. Let me show you the archive, Nathaniel."

She led them to the cluttered, dim and quirky library with its too-bold seventies colors and its chaotic stacks of books and papers. Lillian almost thought the stacks had multiplied since she'd last been inside.

"One of the things we can do," Bethany offered, "if you're both up for it, is connect which of the books the press published directly tie in to local lore, as a joint project with the Historical Society."

"As long as we don't have to open any demon boxes in the process," Lillian replied.

"Yes, let's not."

"If there are wounds this place has had a hard time healing," Bethany continued, "Maybe that kind of work could be a salve."

Lillian nodded. "That's a lovely idea. In the same way that Nathaniel and me, reconnecting with the memories of William and Camille, proves an antidote to the curse." Lillian smiled. "See? Hope left in the bottom of

Pandora's box after all."

Later, entwined with Nathaniel by the carriage house fire in partial undress, the terrors of the day needing some passion as a counterbalance, Lillian posed a question. "Should we switch? Should I stay up there in the mansion and you stay here? This was, after all, your home."

"No, hold down my fort here. This place called to you as a haven and if I'm here, William might influence me too much. We both need to figure out those boundaries between them and us."

"Fair."

"I'll hire a crew to put things in storage in Chicago, have a couple of my buddies watch over the process. I don't have much stuff anyway. I never felt like anywhere was home."

"I know that feeling."

"I don't know if this place is home but... you... You. Whatever this is..."

"Has felt like more of home than I've ever known."

"Yes. And I want to really get to know you. The real you. Whatever of Camille is in there, and whatever of William is in me, we'll get to know all of it and keep what we like and discard what we don't. How does that sound?"

"It sounds perfect."

He gestured to the bandage from his temple to his cheek and spoke dramatically. "If I'm forever scarred by a demon, will you mind?"

Lillian snorted. "When I was a teenager, I wrote a thousand-page fanfic about *The Phantom of the Opera*. I *promise* I won't mind."

Nathaniel laughed. "Now *that* I'd like to read."

"Oh, no. There's a reason I turned to non-fiction."

"After all we've been through, I'm not sure where that line is anymore."

"True. If, after a while here, it ever becomes too much--"

"Then we get out. Just like William and Camille planned. We don't let anyone else, or any weird paranormal forces, tell us what we can or cannot do."

"You're not, though..." Lillian began a bit inelegantly, trying to find the words. "I just want you to know, you're not stuck with me. This isn't predestination. We, our modern selves, have free will. I'll be ok, and you'll be ok, if this doesn't work out. Full disclosure. I'm saying this as much as a pep talk for myself as anything, because I'd be really sad--"

"Agreed. No one is stuck. But I'd be just as sad if we bailed on this. Because I'd like to prove a different thesis in my work this time."

"What's that?"

"*Our* ghost story isn't just a haunting." He pulled her close. "It's a second chance."

She smiled, her heart swelling with hope and satisfaction. "It is. Let's try to get it as right as we can." She tucked deeper into his hold, placing her ear against the thrum of his heartbeat.

"It's all anyone can ask of us," he replied softly, kissing her head. "Past, present or future."

Lillian felt finally confident she could exist now in all of those previously conflicted dimensions at once, boldly and bravely, finally home.

ABOUT THE AUTHOR

Leanna Renee Hieber is an actress, playwright, ghost tour guide and the award-winning, bestselling author of Gothic, Gaslamp Fantasy novels such as the *Strangely Beautiful, Magic Most Foul, Eterna Files* and *The Spectral City* series. Her speculative fiction novellas in the *Time Immemorial* and *The Spirit Suitor* series can be found exclusively via Scrib'd.com in digital and audio editions with Leanna narrating. Her first non-fiction book, *A Haunted History of Invisible Women: True Stories of America's Ghosts*, co-authored with Andrea Janes, focuses on haunted house and ghost stories where women's narratives are centered. A 4-time Prism award winner and Daphne du Maurier award finalist, Leanna's books have been selected for national book club editions as well as translated into many languages. She has been featured in film and television on shows like Mysteries at the Museum and Beyond the Unknown, discussing Victorian Spiritualism. She lectures around the country on themes of Gothic fiction, 19th Century history and the Paranormal for prominent institutions such as New York University, Miami University, and Morbid Anatomy. She is represented by Paul Stevens of the Donald Maass Literary Agency. leannareneehieber.com

CASTLE BRIDGE MEDIA RECOMMENDS...

If you liked *Ghosts of the Forbidden*, you might also enjoy reading the following titles from Castle Bridge Media available on Amazon or by order at your favorite book store:

Austinites
By In Churl Yo

Bloodsucker City
By Jim Towns

**THE CASTLE OF HORROR
ANTHOLOGY SERIES**
Volume 1
Volume 2: Holiday Horrors
Volume 3: Scary Summer Stories
Volume 4: Women Running From Houses
Volume 5: Thinly Veiled: The 70s
Volume 6: Femme Fatales*
Volume 7: Love Gone Wrong
Volume 8: Thinly Veiled: The 80s
Edited By Jason Henderson and
In Churl Yo
*Edited By P.J. Hoover

**Castle of Horror Podcast
Book of Great Horror:
Our Favorites, Top Tens
and Bizarre Pleasures**
Edited By Jason Henderson

Dream State
By Martin Ott

FuturePast Sci-Fi Anthology
Edited by In Churl Yo

Isonation
By In Churl Yo

MID-LIFE CRISIS THRILLERS
18 Miles From Town
By Jason Henderson

THE PATH
The Blue-Spangled Blue
By David Bowles
The Deepest Green
By David Bowles

SURF MYSTIC
Night of the Book Man
By Peyton Douglas

Nightwalkers: Gothic Horror Movies
By Bruce Lanier Wright

**Yesterday's Tomorrows:
The Golden Age of Science Fiction
Movie Posters**
By Bruce Lanier Wright

Please remember to leave us your reviews on Amazon and Goodreads!

THANK YOU FOR SUPPORTING INDEPENDENT PUBLISHERS AND AUTHORS!
castlebridgemedia.com